I0552951

CLACKAMAS LITERARY REVIEW

20th Anniversary Issue

Clackamas Community College
Oregon City, Oregon

CLACKAMAS LITERARY REVIEW

Managing Editor
Matthew Warren

Associate Editors

Marlene Broemer	Trista Cornelius	Sean Davis
Trevor Dodge	Jeff McAlpine	Nicole Rosevear
	Amy Warren	

Assistant Editors & Designers

Nicholas Allison	Tom Boggess	Sam Cassidy
Abigail Cramer	Samantha Dahl	Jack Eikrem
Ashley Goolsby	Becky Lauer	Victoria Marinelli
Delilah Martinez	Jake Parker	Jonathan Ramirez
Naomi Smith	Tania Stavrum	Sabrina Stout
Chelsea Thiel	Denise Tucker	Hollyn Walston
	Joseph Westfall	

Cover Art
Canopy by Alison Dougherty

The Clackamas Literary Review is published annually at Clackamas Community College. Manuscripts are read from September 1st to December 31st. By submitting your work to CLR, you indicate your consent for us to publish accepted work in print and online. Issues I–XI are available through our website; issues XII–XX are available on our Submittable, and through your favorite online bookseller.

Clackamas Literary Review
19600 Molalla Avenue, Oregon City, Oregon 97045
ISBN: 978-0-9796882-9-4
Printed by Lightning Source
www.clackamasliteraryreview.org

CONTENTS

PROSE

"My Friend's Divorce" and "Why the Silence Still Hangs Over Eastern Oregon," by Naomi Shihab Nye, first appeared in the Spring 1997 issue.

"Some Extensions on the Sovereignty of Science," by Alberto Rios, first appeared in the Fall 1998 issue.

"Kansas," by Stephen Dobyns, first appeared in the Fall 1998 issue.

"Kansas" also appeared in *Best American Short Stories of 1999*, edited by Amy Tan and published by Houghton Mifflin. It was published again in *Eating Naked*, from which it was adapted into the short film *Backroads*, by F. Brian Scofield, director and editor, for Over-Soul Films and shot in Lockhart, Texas, in the summer of 2006.

"Idaho Surprise," by Julie Weston, first appeared in the Fall 1999 issue.

"The Saved," by Joe Hill, first appeared in the Spring/Summer 2001 issue.

"The Widow's Breakfast," by Joe Hill, first appeared in the Spring/ Summer 2002 issue.

"Days After," by Patricia Colleen Murphy, first appeared in the 2005 issue.

"Possible Side Effects," by Matthew Roberson, first appeared in the 2006 issue.

"The Parable of the Gun," by Stephen Graham Jones, first appeared in the 2007 issue.

"In Motion," by Paulann Petersen, first appeared in the 2013 issue.

"Child Care," by Margaret Malone, first appeared in the 2016 issue.

Editors' Note

Home is more than place. It is a coming together of people, a safe space to explore ideas—a state of mind we take with us when we go where we go. Opening this book, you are *home*.

For twenty years, the *Clackamas Literary Review* has been such a space. A sanctuary for poets and writers. For stories and their readers. For folks who care deeply about language and narrative in a world that never ceases to discourage and isolate. In honor of this twentieth anniversary issue, we celebrate by housing new literary works alongside work we've previously published.

Here at the *CLR*, college students of all ages and backgrounds collaborate to build a home out of paragraph and page. This year, two days a week we shared our mornings, worked together—to craft *this* book. And as we did, we saw ourselves reflected in its poetry, in its prose. We realize now that we have been making more than just a book. We have been building a place of refuge, where residency requirements are limited only by a willingness to share in the settings constructed, peopled, and furnished by our authors. A place where no one is alone and *all* are welcome. *Home.*

Foreword:
A Conversation with the Founding Editors

Tim Schell and Jeff Knorr

Tim: Jeff, tell me why you came to my office twenty years ago and said, "Should we start a journal or a press?"

Jeff: Well, I suppose I could have come with a different proposal, like "where should we go to get a drink?" In the end, it came from youth and a bit of unbridled ignorance and excitement. I was in the position of feeling like I wanted to be involved in the larger literary community somehow and to do some literary citizen work, the way writers do. I had no idea what it would really take to run a press or a magazine, but I felt like we could manage it somehow and find the money to do it. So, I remember standing in your doorway in the hall while you were sitting at your desk, probably reading some student paper, and asking which we should start—not if we should start one, but which one. You looked at me with utter surprise, then swallowed the Kool Aid and started to ponder which it would be. After deciding on a magazine, I remember taking out our first ad in *Poets & Writers* asking for submissions, and then walking into the mail room a week later and seeing the stacks of submissions we had received and thinking, "Oh man, I had no idea." That was the beginning of five years of non-stop reading.

Tim: Yes, I remember. Man, we created a monster. And then we came up with the idea of creating an annual award, the Willamette Award. I think I read 500 to 600 stories a year just for the award.

Jeff: You know, Tim, you might remember that after two years of that contest we had some discussion of scrapping it. The workload of running that contest was large and felt immense on top of all the other reading for our issues and the editorial duties on top of the reading. If I recall, you were a bit more okay with cutting the contest than I was. I hemmed and hawed and finally called Alberto Rios and had a long talk. I remember Alberto saying one thing that turned things for me. He said, despite the work that it is, when you look back and think about how the award helped writers in their careers (and you may not even know how, but trust it did, he said), you will know you made the right decision to keep the contest. I do believe that contests from small magazines and presses are a vehicle of helping writers in their careers, of validating the work writers do (especially emerging writers) and for that they are a necessary part of the fabric of our national literary community.

Tim: Yes, I remember that. And he was right. On another note, I seem to remember you coming to my office to ask me about what you called "the fuck poem." What was that all about?

Jeff: Ah, "the fuck poem." You know sometimes I would get a poem that I'd look at and think why did this person send this to me. But when I opened the submission from Jonathan Vaile and read that title, "Headline: The Boys' Room" I thought, Hmmm, this ought to be interesting. And, you know, two or three lines in it was clear that it was going to be a well written poem. What I love about that poem is how it unfolds with the surprise of the poem—the surprise not only to the reader but to the speaker of the poem himself. So, it's a very compelling poem because we are captured in the same way the persona is. The word "fuck" is really the least of it; he uses it to effect but doesn't rely on it to carry the poem. In fact, he takes the poem to a very serious level that allows us to see the depth of love in any relationship, homosexual or heterosexual. It's a very good poem for that reason. If I recall though, the question was how we thought the college might respond to the poem if we published it. In the end, nobody said a word.

Tim: Yes, that was a compelling poem, one I think all teachers can relate to.

Jeff: Tim, what is your most memorable moment as an editor?

Tim: The best memories I have as an editor were publishing writers who had never before been published, and publishing them alongside established writers. In our first issue, in the spring of 1997, we published Jim Manuel's surprising story "The Stuffed Dog Man," his first short story, and in the same issue we published a story by the H. Lee Barnes who has gone on to publish highly acclaimed novels and works of non-fiction. In the Fall 1999 issue, we published the story "Kansas" by the renowned writer Stephen Dobyns, and it went on to be published in *The Best American Short Stories*, so of course that was satisfying as well. But the most satisfying moment of editing was publishing Joe Hill's story "The Saved" in the Spring/Summer 2001 issue. Mr. Hill is Stephen King's son, and as he did not want this connection to influence editors, he used the *nom de plume*, and I didn't know of his lineage. Since that publication, he has gone on to publish several award-winning novels. In short, it is highly satisfying to be the conduit of good literature.

A quite different yet certainly memorable moment, I suppose, was reading the beginning of a short story that, after a page, was unreadable, so replete was it with esoteric words that most readers would have to have had a dictionary just to get through the first paragraph (and I have a pretty good vocabulary). I quit reading after one page, but for some reason, I turned to the last page of the story where I saw a handwritten note that said, "if you are too stupid to understand the vocabulary of this story, you probably won't publish it." Well, he was right.

Jeff: So, Tim, you chose a lot of great fiction over the years for the journal. You mentioned both "The Stuffed Dog Man" by one of your students Jim Manuel and the story "Kansas" by Stephen Dobyns. But there were so many others—Lee Barnes, Daniel Chacon, Geronimo Tagatac, Ron Carlson. Tell us a bit about the difference in procuring a piece from a very well-known writer and finding a gem by someone who had not published much (or not published at all) before.

Tim: I was always wary of receiving a story from a well-known writer because what if it didn't make the grade? I think in many ways it was easier to discover a wonderful story by an emerging writer, someone I had never heard of. The one thing that always got me was voice. Sure, plot and character are important, but the writer's voice was always what sealed the deal. And so many of the submissions had compelling voices, it was difficult to find room for everyone. But that's the nature of the game.

Jeff: Tim, can you speak a bit about the early college support for the *CLR* and how that was instrumental in the journal's birth, especially since so many colleges see such projects as outside the mission of a department or ancillary to the benefit of students.

Tim: We were so fortunate to have a supportive English Department and administration. We told them of the importance of literary journals in general, and how this would benefit our own students who wanted to pursue literary lives, and they supported us financially all the while knowing that the journal would not pay for itself...ever. Such support is absolutely necessary, but not always forthcoming. We were lucky.

Tim: Jeff, what one piece of advice would you give student-editors on their first day of the job?

Jeff: Honestly, I would be careful to not give too much advice because I'd really want them to feel their way through the process. But, of course, advice is necessary, and as teachers part of what we do. I suppose there are three things that are important. 1) Be democratic in your reading and editing process. In other words, don't simply read based on your own aesthetic and what you like. What you like doesn't entirely matter. Try to meet each piece you read from a place of craft. Is the author doing things in the poem or story that are effective? Are they trying something new? Is it fresh? What are they trying to do and do you see merit in the work they are putting forward? Being able to approach a work from that place allows us to broaden our taste and experience as we edit. The things we like will always strike us, we'll know those pieces. But if we want to find new voices, original pieces, and fresh writing, then we need to be open to looking at things from outside our normal frame. 2) Know you'll make mistakes. I'm sure every editor who has edited for some time has made some pretty good bungles. It just happens. We miss this piece or that piece, we don't catch something in the proofreading, we get someone's name wrong. Things happen. You might remember when Heather McHugh sent to us and I read her work and, in the end, didn't spend enough time with it. I mean she was, at the time, already well established and an award-winning author. The submission came in over the transom and was in a pile (okay, enough excuses). Anyway, I didn't pay enough attention to the work and I sent it back. I remember dropping the stack in the mail and seeing it go down the mail chute, thinking I should've looked closer. Well, then she gets shortlisted for the Pulitzer a few years later. You know, I'm sure something in that envelope was good enough to publish. We make mistakes. But we learn from them and move on and keep editing. And, I would add for my students, don't let anyone's ire get under your skin—that's just their ego. Finally, 3) Learn from all the writers you read. It's an immense job to edit but there is so much value. I grew so much as a writer during the years I edited at *CLR,* it was just unbelievable. Part of that was reading all of the work that came in and seeing so much happen on the page. But also I created relationships with people who helped me as a writer—Alberto Rios, Kevin Stein, James Hoggard, Lisa Chavez, Marilyn Chin, Virgil Suarez, Walt Mc-Donald. You may remember that Walt and I corresponded a lot, and he gave me some great advice about writing and being a writer. Some of those have lasted as close, lasting friendships.

Jeff: Tim, given that you have taught now for over twenty years at community colleges and universities, what do you think the role of a literary journal is at a college, especially a community college?

Tim: Well, it is certainly making room for voices to be heard, voices that might otherwise be left alone in the woods with no one to listen, but it is also a door for the next generation of editors, poets, and writers to enter and join the literary community waiting on the other side. Young students ought to be afforded as many opportunities as possible, and those aspiring poets and writers and editors at community colleges, given such an opportunity, are the vanguard of a new literary world that we can only visit in our dreams. It is satisfying to know that when our footsteps are swept from the path there are those that follow.

Tim: Jeff, the *CLR* is now twenty years old. If you are to make a toast on its birthday, what would you say?

Jeff: Well, first let me just say that it's a great feeling that *CLR* is twenty and that so many people have worked to keep it going. I'm just thrilled about that. Okay, now for a toast.

Let us celebrate all the writers who have made *CLR* a thriving journal and all the writers who will continue to do so. Let us celebrate the editors who have put their time and love of language into this wild idea. I'm proud to have been one your parents. And I'm honored that so many others have kept you going. To twenty years of voices! Happy Birthday.

Jeff: So, Tim, do you have a toast?

Tim: Sure. Congratulations on your twentieth birthday, and may you continue to thrive. Now, let's hope this is good Scotch. Cheers.

The Lilac Thief

Nick Conrad

—for Gail

Slowly, she steered up the abandoned
driveway; her glance furtive. She fussed
with the seatbelt till, courage screwed in,
she got out and walked to that scented clutch
of purple clouds. 'Like snapping beans,'
she thought, as she broke the twigs. She held

her harvest like a torch. She could see
the vase she wanted to use; how, later,
while stems nursed water, tiny clenched fists
would release an ineffable scent,
part past, part now, that would fuse the scene
to other scenes, the day to other

days, the table suddenly crowded
with those long gone; a dusk fired moment.
So what if, exhausted and empty
handed, those petals later curled and fell,
if, weeks after, a few frail husks
would remain like ashes from some ancient fire.

Called Home

Wynne Hungerford

That day, Joy flushed a dozen pheasants and one porcupine from a field
of cut wheat lightly dusted with snow. Walter had taken Joy, his one-
year-old German Pointer, hunting on his brother-in-law's land outside
Ovando, Montana. Walter didn't like seeing his wife's family anymore,
not with her being gone, but it was good to take a drive and breathe
cold air and watch a bird dog in her element. Of the flushed pheasants,
Walter shot two. Joy carried the birds in her mouth with pure pleasure,
stubby tail wagging, and her confidence ripened with the morning sun.
Walter didn't see the porcupine attack, only heard the dog whine.

He found Joy pawing herself and whipping her head side to side.
Her face was spurred by hundreds of quills. Walter looked in the sur-
rounding brush and saw the porcupine staring at him with polished
black eyes. The mix of brown and gray fur rose like a pompadour
above the rodent's head and fell over the round back. When threatened, they flicked tails covered in hollow, barbed quills. Walter pointed
the gun at the porcupine and said, "I could shoot you," then lowered
the gun. He nodded toward a line of evergreens along the fence-line
and said, "Go climb a tree." He took the old red leash out of his coat
pocket and hooked it onto Joy's collar. She made pained, embarrassed
sounds that Walter understood well.

"I'll take care of you," he said. "But you've got to listen to me
now."

He urged her back toward the car, which was parked a few miles away at the end of his brother-in-law's driveway. Joy wouldn't move. When she licked her lips, Walter worried that she was swallowing loose quills that might puncture her insides.

He said words that she understood: Bronco, home.

After that, Joy gave in.

She didn't know any better than to rush a porcupine. It happened to the smartest of dogs. As a puppy, Joy once slipped out of her collar and bolted down the road after a cyclist. Walter only called her once. Without faltering, she pulled a U-turn and hurtled back to him, soft tongue flying from the corner of her mouth, skinny legs folding and unfolding. It was a miracle, he knew. She was a miracle.

They reached the gate after an hour of hiking. Walter saw his brother-in-law's house, icicles hanging from the TV dish in the front yard. The lights were on, and Walter could have sworn that he smelled bacon cooking, although it was harder to smell in the cold. In the old days, he would have gone inside, taken off his boots for a while, and chatted with his wife's brother, who didn't hunt himself but was proud to make his land available. Not anymore. Walter's small life had grown even smaller with the passing of his wife. He didn't want pity or ridicule. He didn't want small talk. Everything he needed he got from the dog.

In the back of the Bronco, Joy circled and scratched over a pile of old towels and blankets. Walter dropped the game bag onto the passenger seat and cranked the engine. He wasn't going to waste any time warming up his hands or sipping the last of the canteen coffee the way he would at the end of a regular field day. Instead, he shifted into reverse with a numb hand, hardened from thirty-five years of carpentry work, and was about to back out of the driveway when he looked up and saw his brother-in-law Abe walking toward the car. A quick hello was the polite thing to give, but all Walter really wanted was to get home and take care of Joy.

"Howdy-doo, Walt?"

Walter rolled down the window a few inches and said, "My dog's had a porcupine encounter."

Abe peered into the back and saw the damage. He said, "That's some bad luck," and the breath slipped from his mouth like a scarf.

Walter grunted.

"Why don't you bring her on inside?"

"I've got pliers at home."

"We could have coffee or a beer," Abe said. "Do a little catching up."

"I should go."

"You know," Abe said, hands plunged into the pockets of his buffalo-check coat, "we've been family a long time and that doesn't go away just because Nancy's gone. The past, I mean." He squinted and looked over the white fields with patches of gold. "My wife told me to say that," he said. "You know how Celia is."

Walter didn't want people worrying about him, wondering how he'd been since Nancy's death, a year ago, and he sure as hell didn't like anyone saying her name aloud. It gave him a pain in his stomach. He wanted to keep her name, Nancy, and the memory of her face, as soft and lightly browned as sponge cake, safe in his mind.

He drummed his fingers on the steering wheel. He needed to say something appreciative, in case Nancy was listening. Walter said, "Well, thanks."

Abe said, "Come back soon, you hear."

Walter rolled up the window and backed out of the driveway, heading west, away from the wide-open flatness and toward the mountains. The sky was a dirty mirror, and he thought maybe the first real snow of the year was coming soon. Up until then, it had only been light flurries that came in the steely night. He counted the deer sleeping in holes along roadside fences. He watched the odometer roll to 300,000 miles and thought how quickly the miles racked up, how quickly it was over. It seemed like he'd just stolen a pinch of his grandfather's snuff, learned to drive a stick-shift, and seen Nancy for the first time at a spring dance at the Elks Club. Her blonde hair was pinned up like soft-serve ice cream and as they danced, pieces fell from the careful arrangement. She blushed. He said, "I like it both ways," meaning the hair pinned up and also the hair falling free. When he touched her lower back, it felt like a strong slate of marble beneath the cotton of her dress. They sipped lemonade and avoided eye contact for as long as possible until, finally, their eyes met and they blinked and looked away smiling. It seemed as if Nancy had just died, and, days after the funeral, he'd just gotten a ten-week-old puppy to keep himself company.

Out in the field, with the porcupine, Walter hadn't felt that something bad was coming. He never did. That kind of intuition belonged to women more than men. Nancy had known that something bad was happening to her, even mentioned it over breakfast one morning, but Walter hadn't sensed a thing. She'd asked, "Do you believe me?" and he'd said, winking, "I think you're crazy is what I think," and she'd said, "I'm making an appointment."

It was in her ovaries, her bowels, her bladder.

It was passing through cell walls.

It was like the time winter came so suddenly that all of the orange and red leaves froze on the trees in the neighborhood, crystallized.

Back in Missoula, the temperature was falling. Walter led Joy into the house, a brick two-bedroom in the slant-streets. His cheeks burned inside, and, with the heater going, he began to sweat under his coat, sweater, and Pendleton flannel. Joy sat on the living room rug, where she continued pawing her face. She had managed to brush out a fair number of quills on her own, and now they stuck in the rug like tooth-picks half-dipped in black paint. Walter knew that removing all of the quills was going to be a long, difficult task, but he also knew that Joy would not hate him for it. Afterward, she would be grateful. The vet was closed on the weekend anyway, and he wanted to get out as many quills as possible. Monday he could take her for an examination of her mouth and throat. She would be fine, he reminded himself. She would be just fine.

First, he went back to the Bronco and picked up his game bag, holding the pheasants, and brought that inside and put the birds in the refrigerator. The shotgun he returned to the gun rack in the laundry room. Then he found a pair of pliers in one of the kitchen drawers, among loose playing cards, butterscotch candies, and the half-burned candles from Nancy's last birthday, candles in the shape of a large 5 and 9, with bits of frosting hardened on the wax, and returned to Joy in the living room.

He said, "Let me see you."

When Walter spoke, Joy wagged her tail. He sat on the floor cross-legged and groaned like a man of eighty. He was sixty-two. He pulled Joy close and said, "I'll try to work fast." He pinched the pliers around one of the longest quills emerging from the soft brown muz-zle and yanked. That one was loose, easy. "I'm here," he said. "I've got you." Others were deeper in the flesh and required muscle. Joy squirmed against him and pawed one of the buttons off his shirt and even scratched his neck with her toenails, drawing blood. Every time she broke free and ran to the bedroom closet to hide, Walter got up and dragged her back to the living room, designated plucking grounds, and tried again.

While he worked, he said, "You're a good girl. You're a patient girl." As time went on, his mind wandered. He asked, "Do you remember being a puppy? Do you remember your mother and father?" She whimpered. He said, "I wish you and Nancy could have met," and then the dog broke free, and Walter covered his face with his large hands, breathing deeply. He could smell Joy on his hands, the earthy sporting smell of her. Walter wiped his face, stood again, and retrieved the dog. His knees grew hot. After two hours, she almost looked like her normal self again. Red pearls of blood rose from the worst punctures, which Walter dabbed with a kitchen towel.

"It's done," he said. "You did good."

He went into the kitchen and refilled Joy's ceramic dishes with fresh tap water and kibble. She didn't pay any attention to them. Instead, she crawled onto her corduroy pillow in the bedroom. When Walter changed into his pajamas, a soft navy tartan, she lifted her head to listen but wouldn't open her eyes.

Walter said, "'Night," and switched off the light.

In the warm bedroom, they breathed and dreamed in concert.

In the end, there wasn't anything for Walter to do. He couldn't take care of Nancy, the job had gotten too big. The nurses did the bathing, changing, and medicating. Her food came through a tube. Her hospital room smelled like the abscessed port in her stomach, like pus and rot, and one afternoon while she was asleep in the bed and Walter slouched in the corner chair, not asleep but with his eyes closed, somebody paused in the doorway and said, "That shit *stinks.*" Walter's eyes popped open, and he saw a scrawny orderly move out of the doorway. Walter followed him into the elevator where they stood side by side, not speaking, as the orderly picked at a seedy wart on the pad on his thumb. Walter became anger in the shape of a man, a six-foot man with square shoulders, narrow hips, and strong, shaking fists, all packaged in a suede vest and Wrangler jeans. He felt eggs boiling in his stomach, so many eggs that they bounced against each other and made him swell up, the buttons of his vest pulling tight, and steam rising hotly into his mouth, rushing to meet the thin clamped lips, and then continuing up into his nose where it streamed out in two thin jets. He pushed the orderly's head into the wall, a little mashed pea, and said, "You'll curdle, too, you goddamn prick." He stepped out on the next floor and took the stairs back to Nancy's room.

Abe and Celia came to the hospital those last few days. They brought a shiny heart-shaped balloon and a bouquet of grocery-store sunflowers. The three of them sat around Nancy's bed, and Abe told stories of the camping trips the two young couples had taken together. Walter didn't want to hear about good times from the past, not when Nancy was withered beneath hospital sheets, with a white fleece cap pulled over her head. He controlled himself, though. He didn't show his anger, frustration, or fear in front of Nancy. She liked hearing the stories, anyway. She smiled, and the only thing that kept her lips from cracking was a thick layer of Vaseline, which had also been spread around her fingernails and nostrils and over the dry, pale arches where her eyebrows had been. She rested a hand on her chest in delight. Abe talked about the time they sunned on a riverbank outside of Big Fork, a beach of gray and purple pebbles knuckling their backs, and how somebody sat up, he couldn't remember who, and saw a pair of black bears crossing the river.

Abe said, "Remember how lean they looked? And we held our breath and watched them cross."

"It was me," Nancy said. "I saw them first."

Abe said, "The time the car broke down on the divide. Remember, Nance?"

She said, "I wasn't happy."

"You were a pistol all right." He caught himself about to cry. He said, "My little sister."

Later, Abe and Celia went to get doughnuts and read the newspaper in the cafeteria. While they were gone, that last evening, Walter sat alone with Nancy. He was glad that her brother had been able to be there because they had always been close, but he liked it being just the two of them even more. The blanket was pulled up to Nancy's chin, and she was scanning the ceiling as if there was a great bunch of people up there.

She said, "They're calling me."

Walter asked, "Who?"

Nancy kept looking at the ceiling.

She said, "I'm coming, I'm coming."

Her heart rate began to slow, and then, in the last few minutes, it picked up again. He thought, *this is the heart's final sprint.* When it stopped, Walter looked at her eyes. They were still open, although the blue had gone out of them. There wasn't anything left of her, except the echoing of her last words in Walter's head, the words she had been saying throughout their entire marriage, whether they were heading out to dinner or meeting friends for a beer or going for a walk along the Clark Fork. She was always getting ready in the bathroom or changing her clothes or finding the right pair of shoes. Walter was always waiting by the door. It pained him how those old words were made new again.

The morning after the porcupine incident, Walter made a pot of coffee. Joy followed him into the kitchen and stretched out beneath the table. He turned on the radio and listened to the Farmer's Almanac. He took one of the pheasants out of the fridge and pulled over the trashcan. Joy's ears perked up when she sniffed at the bird. Walter said, "This is our prize," and plucked the bird of its rich brown feathers, the body ticked with lighter and darker brown, along with its starched white collar, and, above, the shimmering metalloid patina of the neck, the purple, green, and blue feathers dropped into the bin along with the red face. The tail feathers were a foot and a half long. The bird, naked, was not stripped of its beauty. As Walter butchered the meat, he thought how pretty the organs looked. He cut the crop out of the bird's neck, careful not to break the translucent sack full of wheat seeds. The crop was the organ that held all of the food before it dropped for digestion. Walter held it in his hand, the size of a plum, and admired the seeds. He put it on the windowsill.

Walter took the pheasant breast and gave it a quick egg wash. Then he dropped it in a bowl of flour, covering both sides. He pan-fried the breast and reheated some leftover biscuits. The pheasant browned. He plated a biscuit and half of the fried breast for Joy. She took it between her teeth, snapped it between her jaws. It was amazing how much good a night's rest did, how much healing she had already done. He said, "Is it good?" She wagged her tail. For himself, Walter made a biscuit sandwich with a little coarse mustard and sipped his coffee. He sat at the table and felt Joy nuzzle his leg.

With soft eyebrows she said, "Thank you."

She said, "I love you."

She said, "More?"

He gently took hold of her ears and said, "We'll go for a walk when I'm finished."

She knew the word "walk" and immediately ran for the front door. Her body, a velveteen coat of brown and speckled gray, danced. She jumped and pawed the door and yipped. Outside, a foot of fresh powder covered the old, familiar world.

Hanging Laundry

Donald Levering

A year ago she fell
only to rise later as smoke.
Again I have to lift her
with the week's damp trappings

from my basket to sun and air,
for this is when, reaching
for clothespins, I'd call her.
Her voice when she picked up

would sound older and more frail
than I wanted her to be.
Comparing weather was easy airing,
but queries about her health

she'd hardly answer,
and the talk would veer
to my niece's piano recital
or my nephew's admission to Harvard.

She'd clear her throat to ask,
How's your gang?

I couldn't brag about my son's
recovery—she'd never heard

the dirty part of the story—
dared not report my daughter's
abortion. So I breezed through
the divorce, made light

of my denied promotion
as she listened in silence.
Then I'd let Mom go
and hurry inside.

My eyes would still be trying
to adjust to the dark
when I'd find a wet sock
balled in the bottom of my basket.

A River So Long

Kate Gray

I wish I had a river
I could skate away on
                    —From Joni Mitchell, "River," *Blue*

1.

My mother took in strays, drug-addled
cousins, killing themselves. Instead of coyotes
howling in the hills, sobbing broke my nights
like ice in spring. My mother
listened evenly
to their stories. She prayed. She crocheted.
She required Sunday mass.
Our shoulders touched when kneeling
side-by-side.

2.

These cousins dried
like milkweed pods poking
through snow, their
seed and silk already
tossed to the autumn wind.

3.
Radiators knocked, their heat wet
and unpredictable. Winter's chill pressed
a cold hand suddenly on the neck. I huddled
beneath blankets and listened to "River" over
and over.

4.
After an aneurism dropped my aunt, her oldest
daughter withered to 70 pounds, unable
to lift her children. My mother
plucked her from the hospital.
On the living room floor
my cousin tucked her knees
into her ribs sticking out
while my mother sat in her chair facing
the fireplace, her drink
on the side table, needlepoint in lap. I sat
on the cold floor with my cousin, still so pretty

I couldn't look at her. She didn't say anything to me.
I didn't say anything to her.
At night Joni Mitchell played loud enough
for both of us.

6.
I carried those notes
in my throat to college. My bones
still soft, I started rowing so hard

I pried open
my ribcage
to make a boat fly.

7.

On those winter nights
when I shivered under blankets
and the radiator hissed and gurgled,
when my cousin was vomiting
down the hall, what did I know,
what did I know of cold or what seeds
need to break their sleep?

Why the Silence Still Hangs Over Eastern Oregon
first published in *Volume I*

Naomi Shihab Nye

In the picture
one shoulder of Chief Young Joseph
droops lower than the other
"Due to a childhood injury falling
from a horse."

Maybe.

An interpreter kneels
beside him as a woman in a huge skirt
conveys bad news.

I hope the words hurt her throat.
I hope she was forced to repeat them
till her whole tongue burned.

He who had grown up with talkative rivers
valleys, green mountains
wearing delicate cloud-caps
had to tell his people next.
He had to tell his people.

White tipis at Willowa
shine in the lake's dark eyes.
To this day it is impossible to gaze
into that water easily.

Chief Young Joseph did not like Kansas
one bit.
He said: "I think very little of this country."

What We Knew

Heather Anne Charton

Mrs. Gockley got into making fireworks shortly after her husband passed. She said she was bored. We knew she was trying to blow herself up.

Mr. Gockley had been the chemistry teacher at Eastville High for as long as most of us could remember. He went to Wendy's every day for lunch even though he had to drive past his own house to get there. Mrs. Gockley said she never minded, that she liked the time alone. We knew it drove her crazy.

He'd come into the restaurant wearing his bright white lab coat, black dress pants, and spit-shined dress shoes. He'd order chili and a small Frosty. "Just a small," he'd say. "Have to watch my Wendy-ish figure." He'd laugh and pat his bowling ball beer-belly. He was always five minutes late to his afternoon class. Some of us had taken the class just for that reason—some of us liked an extra five minutes at lunch, too. But most of us had avoided that slot. We hadn't wanted to be short-changed on entertainment. Mr. Gockley was infamous for setting off the school fire alarms. Mrs. Gockley said she thought his antics were amusing. We knew she was embarrassed by it all.

After Mr. Gockley finally succumbed to his high blood pressure and big heart, Mrs. Gockley wore a lemon yellow dress to the funeral. She said she was celebrating his life by wearing his favorite color. We knew she'd simply lost her mind.

So when she started puttering around the shed back behind her house, we tried to keep a close eye on her.

We appointed Billy Vickers as our guardsman. Ever since his retina had dislodged in the garbage truck accident, he'd been sitting at home with nothing to do but collect disability. He nobly took up the cause of keeping his good eye on Mrs. Gockley. They shared a backyard, so Billy could sit on his back porch, sip at his Coors Light, and stare, right past his bird feeder, at Mrs. Gockley's shed.

"How's the bird watching coming, Billy?" she'd ask. He'd wave his notebook at her.

"Three black-capped chickadees, four tufted titmice, and one house finch until a nasty old blue jay scared them all away." His bird counting was his cover. He told her that he submitted his findings to the agricultural research facility up the road.

"Those blue jays have always been bullies," she'd lament and go back to her fireworks.

We asked Billy if he was scared that she might blow him up too, but he said, seeing as he couldn't work, he didn't have much else to live for anyway. So he watched her and reported to us.

"You want to know what I'm working on?" she asked Billy a month or so into his observations. It was July, and the sun was making it harder for Billy to pay attention to Mrs. Gockley. He'd tried wearing a hat to protect his bald head from the sun, but that made him too warm, which made him drink more Coors Light, which made him tired, which led to napping in the afternoon when he should have been watching over Mrs. Gockley. One of us found him an old beach umbrella and helped him strap it to his lawn chair. That seemed to help with most of his problems, but he was getting bored all the same. From where he sat, all he could see was her mixing some white powders with black powders. On the worst days, she would come out early in the morning and put out her little spinning machine—"looks like a flower pot that rolls over and over," as Billy reported—dump some things into it, and set it to rumbling all day long. She'd pop out to check on it once or twice, but other than that, nothing happened except for that obnoxious droning noise.

So when Mrs. Gockley asked Billy if he wanted to know what she was working on, he said yes even though it broke our code. (We knew that if we looked too interested, she'd become all the more intent on blowing herself up.)

She opened the doors of the shed to reveal shelf after shelf of neatly stacked plastic tubs—"Now this is strontium carbonate, which I mix with copper oxide over here to make purple. And this, over here by itself, is sodium benzoate, which can't get near just about anything else because it'll cause a moisture problem. And this here is potassium chlorate, which I keep over here opposite from sulfur because when the two of them get together, well." She leaned in close, conspiratorially, and whispered, "Boom."

Billy said that whisper was scarier than any shout could have been. He wanted to go back to his porch—he wasn't bored anymore—but she had her hand hooked through his arm and was pointing out more things. Next to the stacks of chemicals were netted racks with row after row of little ashy looking squares.

"These are stars," she said.

Billy said her eyes were looking glassy by then. She was smiling just a bit too much for his liking.

"They're what make the lovely colors. These right here," she said, picking one up, "are Bleser KP Red #1. It's a little pinker than I would like, but maybe I'm just being too particular." She got excited then, licking spittle-covered lips. "Why, I could use your help. I'll just light one of these here little fellows right up, and then you can tell me about the color."

"Mrs. Gockley, you don't need to go to all that trouble just for me—"

"Nonsense. It would be a great help to me," she muttered as she began wadding a couple of the stars up in newsprint. She grabbed a lighter and dragged Billy out to the middle of her lawn where there were a couple of scorch marks in the grass. She dropped the crumpled package and then lit the edges of the newsprint.

"Mrs. Gockley! Shouldn't we be running or something? Isn't that what all them firecracker wrappers tell you to do? Light and get away. Why ain't we getting away, Mrs. Gockley?"

The newsprint burned slowly down. Mrs. Gockley patted poor Billy's arm.

"Those are exploding fireworks. This here will just be a flash of color as long as it lights."

Billy didn't seem to have much choice but to believe her, so he slapped his hands over his ears and stood with her. There was a gasp of air as something caught fire and then a soft *poft* and a flash of bright red light. No bang, no disastrous fireball.

"It did look a little pink, didn't it?" Billy admitted. He had to. He shrugged his shoulders in resignation when he told us about it later. "It just don't seem dangerous," he told us. We knew he had caught Mrs. Gockley's madness.

Soon enough, Mrs. Gockley was sitting on Billy's porch under our umbrella, drinking Coors Light, and talking formulas. Soon enough, Billy was huddling with Mrs. Gockley by the shed, fussing with powders, and wrapping up mortar shells.

Ms. Birken was our next line of defense. She was an old farm girl, never married, lived alone with her decaying Old English Sheepdog. She was tough and practical. We all admired her. She and Mrs. Gockley had always been friends of a sort, so we encouraged Ms. Birken to ask her out for lunch or grocery shopping. Perhaps a cup of tea?

"A cup of tea?" Ms. Birken had scoffed. "Just how old do you think I am?" Then she'd patted down her white hair, straightened her pearls, and agreed to our plan.

Ms. Birken asked Mrs. Gockley out to lunch, and Mrs. Gockley agreed—a sure sign, according to Ms. Birken, that Mrs. Gockley was not obsessing over her fireworks. We were less certain.

They went to The Blue Plate, the diner that served early bird specials all day long. Ms. Birken had the ham salad sandwich, and Mrs. Gockley ordered the tuna melt. They each had coffee, but Mrs. Gockley added two creams to hers.

"So what is all this I hear about fireworks?" Ms. Birken asked. She had always been blunt and straightforward. We knew then that we should have started with her instead of Billy.

Mrs. Gockley "giggled." That's the word that Ms. Birken used.

"Oh, Sally," Mrs. Gockley said. "I just needed something to do. Larry had taught me a lot over the years. Told me I had a natural aptitude for chemistry. We'd always talked about making fireworks together someday when he retired."

"But what makes you do it so much? Seems you spend all your time doing it. At least that's what I hear." You had to appreciate Ms. Birken. She kept at things, dogged.

"What else do they expect me to do? Knit and drink tea?"

Then both of them laughed.

Ms. Birken waved her hand at us when she told us. "She's a strong woman. She's not going to sit around doing nothing all because her husband died on her." Ms. Birken shook her finger at us. "You should all be ashamed of yourselves for being so nosy."

Mrs. Gockley was turning out to be a more formidable opponent than we had anticipated.

That was when she announced her big party.

"I'm throwing a wake," she told us at the town meeting.

We were suspicious.

"I'd like to make a tribute to my late husband—a fireworks display containing his ashes."

There was a collective hiss of air sucked in through pursed lips and locked teeth.

But both Billy and Ms. Birken were on the council, so her motion passed. She was granted a permit for her fireworks display. We were left to await the day with grand trepidation.

The week of the wake, we enlisted the big guns to take care of Mrs. Gockley—Fire Chief Barnabas Brightmore. We knew he would be on hand anyway because surely no fireworks display could take place without the fire department. Chief Brightmore was a safety-first kind of man. He'd often annoyed us by denying our use of candles in the banquet hall or closing down the little Italian restaurant for a month because it didn't have illuminated exit signs. We'd found him to be a stuck-in-the-mud stickler. He was the perfect man for the job. We reported all of our findings to him, filtering out Billy and Ms. Birken's eventual approvals, focusing instead on the alarming facts they had provided us with. He readily agreed to protect Mrs. Gockley from herself. He was a public servant after all.

The wake was scheduled to be on Sunday, but it seemed to start on Friday. Mr. Gockley must have done a fine job of keeping in touch with his old students who had moved out of town because they came back in force. We hadn't seen so many vaguely familiar faces in, well, ever. The wake for Mr. Gockley was turning into what Homecoming was supposed to be but never was. As the visitors poured in, the local vendors set up stands and booths all around the town green. You could buy sticky buns and pepperoni rolls from Mrs. Whitmore the baker, funnel cakes from Mr. Ellerbee the owner of The Blue Plate, and creamed chicken sandwiches from the local Boy Scout Troop. The Eastville Athletic Boosters even put together a little bake sale table and ring toss game. Mr. Johnson, from the Depot Bar, scrambled to get permission to set up a beer garden. The Ladies Garden Club put together some funds to upgrade the flower baskets that hung from the street lights. The ones purchased in the spring by the town council had been small and sad-looking, but the new baskets were bursting with blooms of purple and red and pink. They looked a bit like fireworks themselves. The Ruritan club organized a trash cleanup crew that kept the streets looking even prettier than before the influx of visitors. Purr-fect Paws pet groomers, Great Clips hair salon, Ye Olde Shoppe that sold candles and primitives, East of Chicago Pizza, and Hamilton Insurance Office on Main Street washed and polished their plate glass windows until they shone.

We started setting out lawn chairs and beach blankets early on Saturday morning, each of us claiming what we thought would be the best spot to watch the fireworks go off. Mr. Jensen, the high school band director, put together a little jazz band on Saturday evening, and we danced in the town streets until late in the night.

On Sunday morning, we went to church when the bell rang. The minister preached of understanding and love, and we all said,

"Amen." Then the organ started pounding out the postlude, and we flooded back onto the green. It had become a regular fair. But the sight of Chief Brightmore in his somber, sooted gear was sobering for all of us. We knew he had to be sweating profusely under his layers and the mid-August sun, but he looked as stern and granite-like as ever. Mrs. Gockley, surely in an attempt to soften him up, offered some made-from-scratch brownies.

"This was always Larry's favorite recipe," she said as she tempted him.

"No, thank you, ma'am. I'm on the job."

"It's not as if I'm offering you a drink," she countered, pursing her lips in what must have been impatience.

But unflappable Chief Brightmore just tipped his helmet to her and trudged forward to inspect her fireworks display. We couldn't help but follow, our hands full of fair-food treats, our mouths full of laughter.

Mrs. Gockley had constructed her display in the middle of the road just outside of town. Sheriff Loudon was on hand to redirect any traffic, but everyone must have come into town on Friday because there were no cars on the road. The display was smaller than we had anticipated. Its tubes were ordered as if by rank and file. Even the wires running here and there seemed controlled rather than menacing. Chief Brightmore ran his fingers along the fuses. Billy hovered over his shoulder.

"Please stop touching things, Chief. I've worked darned hard to get all them fuses stuck together, and it'd be a crying shame if one of them fell off now," Billy whined.

Chief Brightmore turned and glowered at him. His eyes were charcoal briquettes.

"Of course you need to inspect it all, Chief Brightmore," said Mrs. Gockley. "I understand well enough." She patted Billy's back. "That's all right, Billy. Chief Brightmore here is just doing his job. He wouldn't pull off any of those fuses you worked so hard to put together. Would you now, Chief Brightmore?"

But Chief Brightmore said nothing.

Mrs. Gockley showed him her remote firing system. She told him how she would be sitting on the green with the rest of us when she set them off.

He just kept tracing wires.

The jazz band struck back up on the green, so we left Chief Brightmore to his wires and danced until the sky turned dusky. Then we gorged ourselves on more fair food and settled into our viewing spots.

Someone had found Mrs. Gockley a microphone. She stood in front of us on the edge of the green. Although we'd turned off all of the street lights so that we could see the fireworks better, our eyes had adjusted to the darkness as it swept over us, and they gave us no trouble making out her form. We applauded.

"Thank you all for coming," she called out to us, her voice shining. We strained our eyes to hear better. "This evening, well, this weekend really—"

A round of laughter, some catcalls from the beer garden.

"Has all been for my late husband, Mr. Larry Gockley."

A great roar and a few whistles. It seemed the beer wasn't just in the beer garden.

"He was greatly loved and is dearly...missed."

We saw how much she loved him, and we remembered how much we loved him too. There was a pause, a moment when none of us were certain that she or we could really go on without him.

But Mrs. Gockley was braver than we gave her credit for. She pressed on: "Billy! Where's Billy at? Anyone seen Billy?" She had one hand up over her eyes as though shielding her sight from the glare of the moonlight. Billy's bumbling form appeared from among us, slipping between and around our chairs and blankets. Even in the darkness, we could tell he was blushing, maybe it was the way he hunched his shoulders and tucked his head. He found his way to Mrs. Gockley, and she wrapped an arm around his shoulder and squeezed. She seemed to be holding him up. "Billy here thinks that we should do this every year—"

We clapped and shouted with approval. She waited patiently until we quieted down again.

"And while I can't agree more, I just don't think I have the heart for it. So I'm putting it to all of you. Billy's going to set up a committee next town meeting for an annual fair. I expect he'll have all of your support."

We cheered in agreement.

"And now as soon as Chief Brightmore gives us the a-okay, we'll bring on the main event."

Mrs. Gockley and Billy filtered back into our midst, and we watched the road. We could no longer see the shadows of the fireworks display or Chief Brightmore, but we stared in that direction anyway. The stars seemed to shift, but no one said a word. A few children laughed and screamed as they scampered about, recklessly joyous that they could run down the middle of the street without anyone yelling at them. Then a form appeared, a darkness within the darkness, and the silhouette of Chief Brightmore marched towards us. He stopped where Mrs. Gockley had stood.

"Because the display was put together by a hobbyist instead of a federally licensed professional, I cannot approve the display."

He marched around the green back towards the firehouse.

We sat in silence.

Mrs. Gockley teetered back to the front of our group. "My stars. All that time and an answer like that. I'm so sorry about all of this, folks." She held her hands out to us, an offering of emptiness. "I just didn't imagine there would be so much bother. Now here I've got all of you out and ready for a fireworks show, and I can't give you anything." Her voice was wavering behind what we could only imagine to be tears. We thought of Mrs. Gockley's love for Mr. Gockley. We thought of Mr. Gockley's ashes trapped in those shells. We thought of the fireworks we had been waiting for. The door of the firehouse shutting was louder than any mortar.

"But the town council approved it!" someone from the back called.

"Yeah!" joined another voice.

"No one said the fire chief had to approve it!"

"Let's set them off anyway!"

The crowd was humming now, a gentle wave of rebellion and anticipation rolling through us. One man stood little chance against a town.

"Oh, now, I don't want to cause a fuss," Mrs. Gockley pleaded. The remote firing system for the display was in her hands. We could see the glow of the lit switches. The display was armed and ready to go.

The crowd kept at her, cheering her on. And then there was a *pfzt*. A fuse lit up the darkness down the road. We fell silent and watched the glowing orb snake farther away from us. We held our breaths. There was a wild hiss, and the fuse split off into four directions. More splits, more hissing. Then came the deep bass thud of a mortar going off. The sound hit us deep in our chests so that we grabbed absently at the bases of our throats. We stared up in childlike anticipation—it was the night before Christmas, the first day of college, the wedding rehearsal dinner. We knew that so much lay ahead of us, but we didn't know what. Then the shell burst, even higher than we had been looking. A brilliant crack, a glistening of silver and blue.

"Ahhh," was all that could be said.

Thud, thud, thud.

Crack, crack, crack.

Sparkles of red, bright bursts of purple, a palm of gold.

And then there was a cacophony of thuds and cracks and snaps. The sky bloomed with one flower bursting open over another until there was so much light that it was almost impossible to determine their colors. They banished the night.

The afterglow lasted longer than the fireworks themselves. For a moment we stared at the empty sky, the burn of our retinas filling it with lights that weren't there. It was as if we'd stared down the sun. Then we erupted in an applause as loud as the mortars had been.

"Ambulance!" someone shouted. We silenced. The voice belonged to Billy. We stumbled in our blinded darkness towards him, crowded around him. Mrs. Gockley sat slumped in a lawn chair, a kiddish grin on her face. Billy looked pale.

The doctors later reported that the bursts from the mortars had caused an arrhythmia, inducing a heart attack.

We knew better. We thought of the weekend. We thought of Mr. Gockley. We thought of Mrs. Gockley. We all knew she'd died of a broken heart. And though we were sometimes wrong, sometimes we did know best.

Back

Harry Newman

You have to walk backwards
backwards until you meet yourself

you have to slip into your old skin
it doesn't fit but you can stretch it
stretch it until it tears until it

hangs ripped and red with sores
you have to adjust the skull over yours
breaking bones teeth the tight mouth

puckering muscles slackened with age
this was your mouth the smooth lips
that whispered *help me Lord*

you have to swallow one tongue
you have to breathe the air you
once exhaled air thinned of oxygen

you gasp for breath as you never had
in your brain memories overlap though
incompletely thoughts superimpose

out of phase it's dizzying
to know so much and so little
you have to focus four eyes now

to see the world with two times
double vision then you have to
you have to take a step this is

the hard part to move yourself
forward on legs you've forgotten

Fragile Things

Darius Atefat-Peckham

While playing, I run past an
Ornamental bowl in my grandparents'
House. It sat under my mother's gallery of paintings
That hang in her memory. The bowl was a
Birthday gift of my mother's, my Bibi tells me, one of
Those pieces that my grandparents never had the
Heart to send to Goodwill or gift away, a piece of her life.
My flailing arms clip the sculpted trim and
The bowl splashes like paint on
Canvas; spreading stars of sharpened crystal.
Bibi, my Grandma, (in Farsi
It means lady) limps quickly toward the glass.

Watching her, I am
Reminded of the painting of
My mother's that hangs in the
Building of her former college,
You can take a piece of it.
Keep it in your pocket like it's her,
A professor informs me. It feels wrong,
But the texture's ruined anyways, and his
Pressing hands are grieving on my shoulders

So I take a piece and pocket it.
My eyes widen as it tears.

I watch Bibi fall to her knees and
Let crystal dance through her
Fingers. It strikes me, then, how easily
The fragile bowl had broken. The shards leave her
Thin cuts and I start to cry.
Her lips turn and in her accent,
Don't. It's good. She says thoughtfully
And smiles.

Tenderness

Deborah Keenan

Skating at night alone
the field flooded
no wind no snow
disturbed the calm
freezing and the one
who was once a friend
skated past then circled
then placed his arms
in that old diagonal way
took her hands

The body memories
inside the two who
could not be friends
woke and they came
together circled
the field now perfectly
frozen their blades cut
with only a faint shaping
sound

they did not harm
the ice
they skated and surrendered

to the end of their friendship
serene and shocked
by the winter portrait
they had hoped
never to create.

Possible Side Effects

first published in *Volume X*

Matthew Roberson

Ambien® He knew he should quit smoking.

But everyone lit up while they framed or roofed, and on breaks, and why not? The days were hot or cold, or muggy, or wet, and they struggled, morning to night, Monday to Friday, seven to seven. Not an hour passed without a cut or bruise to their hands and legs. They worked on their knees in tight spaces, drilling and nailing, and stretched to reach beams or lift lumber above their heads. They carried eighty-pound bags of shingles up extension ladders.

Why not take the simple pleasure of a smoke.

Other pleasures were gone. E. limped home nights too tired to cook a real meal, and L. didn't make dinner anymore, either, so they took out, or ordered in, or ate from the kitchen shelves—a can of olives. Six bananas. Canned chili, cold. Hot dog buns. Sex was out, except on weekends, and even then E. found he couldn't be roused. Better to watch cable. Football. Or *Die Hard*, again. He wouldn't follow tennis or soccer or any sport that looked tiring. Who needed it? He turned on baseball, in season, or listened to it on the radio, flat on his back on the living room rug.

But the cigarettes gave him a wet, morning cough, and raw, burned sinuses, and got him up from bed all night, agitated, having to pee, and it was the nicotine—or its absence—that made him antsy. And he couldn't shit before work without coffee and a smoke, so he took them in the toilet, with the paper, and turned on the fan and drank and smoked and waited and grew hemorrhoids. L. yelled about smoking in the house but never rose early enough to stop him.

E. played lacrosse in high school. He knew what it was to be fit. E. was not fit. He felt weathered and stiff.

He asked Dr. U_____ for something for nights, to help with sleep, but Dr. U_____ wouldn't bite. Anything he could give held risks, so he said no, quit smoking if you need to sleep, though nicely, knowing E. would take offense.

As if it's easy to quit, E. said.

He got L. to ask her doctor for a script, which she did, so they had a month's supply of Ambien®, which sat on L.'s dresser. The cat knocked it off, jumping past.

The pills were white with AMB 10 punched in their sides.

L. said this was it. She wasn't asking the doctor for more.

And Do Not Take With Alcohol, she said, because the doctor told her that was out. Contraindicated. And only one a night, L. said. There's Risk of Coma. Risk. Of. Coma. Don't be stupid.

Right, E. said.

Benadryl® Before he got the Ambien, E. tried taking Benadryl, popping two back before bed, but they wore off at three, maybe four a.m., and he would wake sweating and confused, thirsty, and mix a jug of orange juice and lie restless on the sofa.

Caffeine Mornings he knocked his way to the kitchen, where the coffeemaker sat in clutter, to brew a pot of dark blend before heading to the can (see **Ambien**).

Midmornings, he got a large coffee from McDonalds or 7-Eleven and stirred in sweetened creamers, if he could. Irish Creme, Hazelnut. Ditto, afternoons.

His legs shook on ladders, and a thick munge of brown coated his tongue. He had acid reflux.

Darvocet® You gotta clear the decks for eight solids, E. told Tim, about Ambien. That shit puts out the lights, he said, and even after a ten to six stretch he still floated through the a.m., his brain too slow for power tools, and his fingers coming off in the circular saw hurt like a pinch and then a tug, and then just hurt. Only two, but still. He wrapped his hand and asked Tim for his soda—the cup and the ice—and gathered his fingers and got Edward to drive him to Baptist Memorial, where they sewed him up, splinted his hand past the wrist, and made free with Darvocet. He paid the fifty dollar fee. He went home for the afternoon.

For a while, he laid off Ambien. He had Darvocet for nights.

Ex-Lax® For lunch, the crew got McDonald's/Burger King/Wendy's/Subway/Popeye's/Jersey Mike's/Taco Bell/Jack in the Box. Later, if E. and L. bought dinner, they got pizza or fried chicken. Sometimes a salad side, with blue cheese dressing.

E. burned it off, and L. gained weight, and got mad, and smashed a dinner plate, and cried, because she was supposed to sit all day and then eat like a construction worker and not be as fat as a house? She needed E. to help. If they were going to get takeout, she said, it should be from the Kroger deli. Roasted chicken, no skin. Or fish. Rice, and vegetables.

You don't like fish, E. said, and L. gained more weight, and E.'s guts clogged (see **Ambien** and **Caffeine**). On the worst days, he took laxatives and hunched through breaks in a porta-pottty, if their site had one, or on a crapper in the nearest store. At a bodega on Fourth, E. took too long, and the owner entered, his shoes showing through a break under the stall door. He stood for a minute before he spoke. You all right?

Fluoride To clear the munge from his mouth and tongue (see **Caffeine**), E. scrubbed with **MentaDent®**. Twice through his molars and onto the front teeth and across his taste buds until they burned.

Gaviscon® He didn't like how it foamed in his mouth, but it helped after lunch, when burgers lodged in his windpipe and he burped onions.

Head & Shoulders® Probably he should have used a gentler shampoo. His hair was thinning, and two shiny patches of scalp grew backward on the sides of his forehead. But he hated dandruff. He found it embarrassing.

Ibuprofen Two 500 mg. capsules didn't cut the pain like Darvocet, which was long gone, ditto the Tylenol® with Codeine, and the Percocet®. It didn't help that he worked his hand all day, managing whatever didn't need fine motor skills. He lifted, hauled. He held beams while they were nailed in place. He learned to handle the nail gun with his left hand, and L. had no sympathy about the pain because, one, he wasn't supposed to use his hand for six weeks, and, two, if he used it, it wasn't going to heal right, meaning, three, he'd have more problems down the road, and, four, if he could frickin haul lumber with it he could get his own drink from the fridge. Put down the bag of chips or come back. She had enough work without having to wipe his butt, and she wasn't getting up at six anymore to help with his mornings. Maybe if he made more money, she could cut back to part time, and she could help around the house, and they could have time for other stuff, too.

Just Tears® He gave contacts a try, because L. said to, meaning, E. knew, if she caught him popping the stems of his glasses in his mouth again, to suck off the sweat, she'd scream, but he forgot to take the lenses out at nights, and he got a corneal scratch, and glasses worked better at stopping wood chips and dust. So back to the horn-rims with a Croakies® strap.

Kaopectate® What Scott said, when he saw E. pull out a bottle, was the main ingredient was dirt or some such shit. Kao-Pectate, he said. Kao, he said. Kao-lan or lin or lon, he said. Look at the ingredients. It's clay. Bismuth subsalicylate 525 mg, E. said. Caramel, carmethylcellulose sodium, flavor, microcrystalline cellulose, purified water, sodium salicylate, sorbic acid, sucrose, titanium dioxide, and xanthan gum. Lemme see, Scott said, and E. started buying Imodium®, which came in tablets and worked better at stopping what Ex-Lax started.

Lamisil® The stink that came from E.'s feet when he peeled off his socks. Cat piss. It was fungus and sweat. L. wouldn't let E.'s boots inside, and, when they smelled up the porch, she threw them out.

E. didn't always wear clean socks because he didn't like washing the pile of clothes blocking his closet, because that meant a trip to the basement at night or on weekends, so he ignored the mess until L. washed five or six loads and dumped clean stuff on the bed. If he wanted to sleep, he folded.

Lamisil cream would have killed the fungus, but he didn't use it regularly, most times, and when he did, he forgot to pour bleach on the shower floor, which only got clean when L. caught athlete's foot and yelled at him and scrubbed for an hour. She threatened to spend their money on a cleaning lady.

Maalox® At least it acted fast. Didn't help for long enough. Dense, like a milkshake. Chalky. (See **Gaviscon**).

Nicotine In college, when E. and L. both smoked, they could cloud a room in minutes. In E.'s apartment. Not L.'s. She didn't like how the smoke lingered in her towels and drapes.

E. bought packs of Camel Lights® for L. and left them in her coat, for her to find when he wasn't around. Matches he left, too, or a lighter, and L. always meant to do the same for E., but, absent-minded, forgot. That was okay.

When E. quit school and moved into L.'s place, they took to stepping out back, onto the balcony.

After L. graduated, she quit. She didn't want to become a pariah at work, huddling outside around sand-filled ashcans. And she needed to be healthy to have babies someday. So.

E. kept smoking with the guys at the job (see **Ambien**), and it cost more than he and L. could afford, almost thirty bucks a carton.

If E. couldn't find an ashtray or didn't want to ash in the grass, he rolled his pants and flicked into the cuffs. If there was no place to put his butts, he pinched off the red ends and pocketed the filters. Come laundry time, he and L. fought over the mess.

Oxycodone with APAP By law, he could have five days of Darvocet. After that, the doctor wrote him a script for the same thing, different name: Tylenol with Codeine. After that, a heavy dose of Ibuprofen (see **Ibuprofen**).

E. decided that for re-attached fingers, Ibuprofen didn't cut it. The guys at work agreed, and Tim scored him two dozen Percocets in original wrappers.

E. hated the stitches sitting below his knuckles. They looked like wiry eyelashes. Spider's legs. At night, before he fell asleep, he could feel his fingerbones rejoining.

Pseudoephedrine Until he dropped out of college, E. took Wal-Phed® to cram for exams and stay sharp in class and just give a lift. He lost ten pounds. He felt on edge and smoked more and wanted to smash in the heads of kids wearing sweatpants to class. Smug, little cunts. Baseball caps on backwards. Never worked a day in their lives, E. figured. They could use some hard knocks.

E.'s dad said to go. He said E. didn't want to spend his life working shitty jobs. It's too hard, he said. Later on, when you get older. Look at your old man, he said. Right out of high school, roofing didn't seem so bad. For a couple of years. But use that money for college, E.'s dad said, so E. did, at 23, when he was older than most seniors. His parents bought his books.

Two years later, when he quit, they promised to help again, whenever, and L. said she would too, because they were thinking about marriage. Go back when I get a job, she said, knowing he wouldn't, and it would be a problem, someday, his lack of options. But, then again, who knew, maybe he would move up, or start a business, and she didn't want his leaving college to mean his leaving her, because she was having a tough time too, she told her mom, with classes, and her major, and everything, though who was she to complain.

She was lonely more often than she liked.

E. kept on with his summer carpenter position and moved in with L. He took over the rent.

About college, E. said he wanted a break. It made him itch, he said.

And he was out of funds.

Quick Pep® Only once did E. mix Quick Pep and coffee. How could extra caffeine be bad, he thought, before his hands developed a slick coat of sweat, and his heart started pounding, hiccupping every few beats, and the world tilted at the damnedest angle, and he fell to his knees, head hanging down, until he could get it together. Dropped a wallboard anchor, he said to Scott. Somewhere around here, he said. Just get another, Karl said, and E. said, Okay. Yeah.

Rhinocort® Hay fever season, four snorts in the morning. It made his nose bleed, but he didn't sneeze. It would have been better if they kept the yard down, which the lease required, but come weekends E. couldn't get himself to mow, and L. was damned if she'd do it and clip the weeds and trim the bushes, so she hired the Branski's kid, David, from down the street. He did a crappy job, once a month, leaving patches of weed climbing their fence. But there you go. If E. wanted it different, he could take care of it himself.

Sominex® Basically Benadryl, the pharmacist told him. An antihistamine.

Fuck that, E. said, later, to L. (see **Benadryl**).

Tylenol with Codeine He kept four, for the future, for who knows what.

Unisom® Basically Benadryl, the pharmacist told him. An antihistamine.

Fuck that, E. said, later, to L. (see **Benadryl**).

Valium® Dr. U_____ said, It's not a good choice. If you wake at night, cut back on caffeine. If you need help to quit smoking, we could try

Wellbutrin®, which curbs your craving.

If you still can't sleep, maybe a non-benzodiazepine. Maybe.

But not Valium, which works for intense periods of anxiety, Dr. U_____ said, like

Xanax®, which is newer. They're very addictive.

Okay, E. said. Though, at night. Even in the day. Like there's something right then. You know?

What do you mean, Dr. U_____ asked.

E. said, What do you mean?

.

E. said, Intense anxiety. Yes. I have intense anxiety.

Yasmin® L.'s doctor gave her a three-month refill, for fewer co-pays. She kept the extra packets in their top bathroom drawer. The pills for the month went in a soft, blue case on her dresser.

She needed to lose fifty pounds. The extra weight put her at even greater risk for heart attack and stroke. With her luck, breast cancer, too. But she didn't like diaphragms, and she didn't trust E. to use rubbers, and they didn't have enough money for kids, and she didn't think they ever would. She'd always have to work, at least. Then, daycare costs.

They couldn't even keep a goddam house clean. No kids, she said to E. Not now, she said. Maybe never, she said. Do you care?

L. had a bank account she didn't share with E. She put away a hundred dollars a month, just in case.

Zoloft® Sometimes it's part of a bigger thing, Dr. U_____ said. The sleep. Maybe we want to think about underlying problems. Maybe you need to lift your mood.

There are a lot of good meds out there, Dr. U_____ said. Serotonin builders.

·

What's that, E. said. Antidepressants?

·

You're saying I'm nuts, E. said.

·

I don't need happy pills, E. said.

Just the Xanax, E. said. Or the other one.

I'm fine, E. said. Just fine.

Passage

Sunni Brown Wilkinson

Six p.m. closes in on the plane and the noise and the silence
push against each other. The businessman clutches
his cell phone. The conversation we heard—
She gets a million dollars; I want everything else—

hangs in the air around him. At the back, a baby cries
as if its mother is not there, though she has been there
all along: rocking, humming. You are next to me,
and Lake Michigan is below.

High up in this moving room with strangers
we are close and you are quiet
and more than ever that boy who lifted
my dying friend last summer

into the sunlight and carried her in your arms
down the long beach so she could hear the waves
and the gulls, so she could watch our boys dig
in the sand with shovels the color of crayons,

so she could try on my life in your arms
and sit in the sun next to her mother

and all afternoon remember herself
weightless and beloved

before she is carried
where she was meant to go.
As we are now.
A fine evening light washes

over our hands
and the worried baby and the man
who is losing everything and the people
already sleeping.

Second Messenger

Lauren Smith

A telephone lets you hear someone's voice removed from her body, separate from her face and eyes. It puts us into pieces from the start.

"What a beautiful arrangement!" I shift the receiver to my other ear. Out the window, I see a ladder on the Bell Atlantic building; workers have pulled down the round, golden disk with the raised image of a bell in the middle and are hanging another in its place. The replacement is smooth with a red line darting across a black field. "Verizon" is a silly name for a company, the analysts I work with say. For this, my first real job out of college, I cut-and-paste research papers about *end-users*, *VoIP*, *local loop*, and *telephony*. This last one sounds like a Greek muse to me. It's 1998.

Bell's old-school cables and switches are carrying the call I'm having now. So much depends on landlines, on dialups. I'm on the phone with my father—he checked himself into the hospital last night because of stomach pains. He doesn't take care of himself. Fat and proud of it. When we went to the shore in the summers, he would expose his big belly to the sun, the burgundy scar from his gall bladder glistening under the water.

This trip to in-patient should be brief. He's probably just dehydrated. The purple, pink, and blue squares in the art print taped to the wall of my cubicle suggest order, and they calm me.

"A beautiful arrangement," he repeats. He's talking about the flowers I sent him. He sounds a little loopy, a little drunk. Why is he saying "arrangement" instead of bouquet? "Beautiful" is a lot of word for a $40 basket of daisies. This is a man who grew up playing stickball. He eats hamburgers plain, and he doesn't like greeting cards with cellophane covers. When I got a B- in Industrial Arts, he shook his head and said he didn't get why a girl was taking shop anyway. But here he is in my ear, three hundred miles away, cooing about beautiful arrangements.

Telephone scientists and brain scientists each describe how their network is fast, so fast we don't even notice it working. They pass energy back and forth, instantaneous and invisible. Each is a web, delicate and able. The voice on the phone asks me how school is. This time he sounds fake and exuberant, like he's on helium except with no change at all in pitch. His normal voice is a baritone, and when he speaks at weddings and funerals, he delivers long pieces of prose over which he never stumbles. When he taught me to read aloud, he insisted I get the phrasing right, making sure my listener could tell how one word led into the next. He also kept a watch on me, getting uptight when I laughed too long, cried too hard, lingered with an idea. When I was nine, he found me talking to cartoon characters on TV, and he grabbed me by the shoulders and demanded to know if I could tell the difference between fantasy and reality. I promised him I could.

"What school? I'm not in any school." He'd been at my college graduation two years ago; he made too many jokes with his ex-wife and her boyfriend. His tan wallet had cracks in the corners, and he dropped it as we were stepping over a curb. He grumbled about the walk across the Common. Why am I grasping at these half-snippets of memory?

I ask how he's feeling. "Feel? Feel? I feel a real peel. Emma Peel. Bell peal. Ringing spud? A potato peeler." His words are rapid now, and they chase an uncatchable rhythm. I wait for a laugh, for him to tell me this is all a goof. Instead, his voice turns flat, and he unleashes a stream of babble, melodic and jagged. He has a reputation as a punster, and everyone says how brilliant he is. "I'm having a confabulation, Dear. Confabulation." I scribble the word on a Post-it. "Gracious, gracious confabulation." And then another wave of nonsense.

Later, I'll learn he is clanging. People in a state of mania get distracted by the sounds of language, and so they clang, putting words together that are alike or rhyme but don't otherwise relate. Shiny linguistics pull their ears, and then their mouths, away. A clanging person is a florist of the cerebrum, grabbing this rose to put next to that peony. Clanging's fun in a nursery rhyme, or a book of poetry, or anyplace where we know it's intentional. But these pealing bells and gracious confabulations don't seem that way to me. They seem like stray pills that have slipped out of the orange bottle Dad always has in his pocket. It rattles as he walks. He takes a couple of pills at each meal with no explanation, jerking his head back to swallow. It's like he wants to make sure he won't have to do it again.

"I love you," I say, feeling cheesy and trying to act out a long-distance commercial from the Eighties. Reach out, reach out, and touch someone. The phone base on my desk has buttons; I could press one and make this voice go away. "Do you hear me? I love you." Maybe his mind will store my message for later, and he can play it back and be comforted. But he only giggles, a Jabberwocky moving his tongue. He whispers something about the Germans knowing where he is, and we hang up.

Like vocal cords, telephone wires work by vibration, transmitting sound from one place to another. Lithium—the medicine he has stopped taking—doesn't make anything vibrate. It treats bipolar through blocking transmissions from some receptors in the brain to others. It lowers the activity of the brain's "second messengers," cells that carry information from one neuron to another. Off his lithium, he could have stimulated too many of these messengers, permitted too many transmissions.

When he recovers in a few weeks, I'll visit. He'll invite me for dinner, and when I see him in front of the restaurant, I'll notice his cheeks have thinned. The skin of his neck will have loosened. We'll hug, and dots of joy will brighten his face. He'll smell of newsprint and aftershave. We'll have a long-overdue discussion about his secret. He'll ask me if I think he's crazy, and I'll deny it. I'll say that bipolar—even his case, which pushes well past the clichés of "mood swings" and into the dreamland of psychosis—is just like any other illness. I'll say this even though I don't believe it or think that anyone else should have to accept it as true.

I need a bigger word for what he is. A fuller word, a more respectful word. One more suitable for what can show me our wiring.

Inside my apartment the night of the call, I play the radio loud so that I won't hear my own phone if it rings. I refold pairs of jeans and make stacks of tops. I sit on the floor and dig my fingers into the plush cords of a green sweater. When I notice what I'm doing, I stand up and go back outside. In the 7-Eleven a few blocks away, I watch strangers buy tuna fish and Tide. Part of me is starting to see how, along with the stories, all the covers of the self, a person is a telephone. A series of signals firing, sending and receiving.

Blood Flowers

Darius Atefat-Peckham

I am told that on her deathbed my
Great-grandmother kissed my picture
Lovingly. Afterward, her shoulders drew away
And she settled into her pillow,
Looking at Bibi's tears for affirmation. She turned away
From her daughter's sorrow and watched birds land on
Telephone wires and fly away like ink spots.

I wonder if she thought of the man she let live
In the shed behind her garden, his children who
Wore my mother's baby clothes, ones that lay
On short tree branches to dry, dripping soap and
Water. After school, the children run screaming
And, giggling, they fall into cement walkways and
Thorns and roses. These kids must have thought
They were in a heaven vast with color and
Hiding places, and maybe they
Noticed when the flowers started to wither, when she
Came out less to tend their color. Or maybe they noticed
The denim overalls shriveling in the sun, unfolded,
An ignored bloodstain at the knee.

The Widow's Breakfast

first published in *Volume VI, Issue I*

Joe Hill

Killian left the blanket on Gage—didn't want it—and left Gage where he lay on a rise above a little creekbed somewhere in eastern Ohio. He didn't stop moving for the better part of a month after that, riding the freights north and east, as if he was still headed to see Gage's best cousin in New Hampshire. He wasn't though. Killian would never meet her now. He didn't know where he was headed.

He was in New Haven for a while but didn't stay. One morning, in the early dark, he went to a place he had heard about, where the tracks swept out in a wide arc, and the trains had to slow down almost to nothing going around it. There he waited. A boy in an ill-fitting and dirty suit jacket crouched beside him, at the base of the embankment. When the northeastern came, Killian jumped up and ran alongside the train, and hauled himself up into a loaded freight car. The boy pulled himself into the car right behind him.

They rode together for a while, in the dark, the cars jolting from side to side and the wheels banging and clattering on the tracks. Killian dozed, came awake with the boy tugging on his belt buckle. The kid said for a quarter, but Killian didn't have a quarter and if he did, he wouldn't have spent it that way.

He grabbed the boy by the arms, and yanked his hands away with some effort, digging his fingernails into the soft undersides of the boy's wrists, and hurting him on purpose. Killian told him to leave be and shoved him away. He told the boy that he looked like a nice kid and why did he want to be that way. Killian said to the boy to just wake him when the train stopped in Westfield. The kid sat on the other side of the car, one knee drawn up against his chest, and his arms wrapped around the knee, and didn't speak. Sometimes a thin line of gray morning light fell through one of the slats in the boxcar wall, and glided slowly up the boy's face, and across his hating and feverish eyes. Killian fell asleep again with the kid still glaring at him.

When he woke the boy was gone. It was full light by then, but still early enough and cold enough so when Killian stood in the half-open boxcar door his breath was ripped away from him in clouds of frozen vapor. He held the edge of the door with one hand, and the fingers that were outside were soon burned raw by the sharp and icy current of the air. There was a tear in the armpit of his shirt, and the cold wind blew through that too. He didn't know if Westfield was still ahead of him or not, but he felt he had slept for a long time—it was probably behind. Probably that was where the boy had jumped out. After Westfield there wouldn't be any other stops until the train dead-ended in Northampton, and Killian didn't want to go there. He stood in the door with the cold wind blasting at him. Sometimes he imagined he had died with Gage, and had wandered since as a ghost. It wasn't true though. Things kept reminding him it wasn't true, like his neck stiff and achy from how he slept, or the cold air coming through the holes in his shirt.

At a trainyard in Lima, a railroad bull had caught Killian and Gage dozing together under their shared blanket, where they were hid in a shed. He had kicked them awake and told them to get. When they hadn't got fast enough, the bull struck Gage in the back of the head with his billy, driving him to his knees.

The next couple days, when Gage came awake in the mornings, he would say to Killian he was seeing double. Gage thought it was funny. He would sit for a while just where he was, turning his head from side to side, and laugh at the sight of the world multiplied. He had to blink a lot and rub at his eyes before his vision would clear. Then, three days after what happened in Lima, Gage started falling down. They would be walking together, and then Killian would notice all of a sudden that he was walking alone, and he would look back and see Gage sitting on the ground, his face waxy and frightened. They stopped in a place where there was nothing, to rest for a day, but they shouldn't have stopped, Killian shouldn't have let them stop. They should have gone where there was a doctor. Killian knew that now. The very next morning Gage was dead with his eyes open and surprised by the creekbed.

Later Killian heard talk at campfires, heard other men tell about a railroad cop named Lima Slim. From their descriptions he guessed that this was the man who had struck Gage. Lima Slim had often shot at trespassers; once he had forced some men at gunpoint to jump off a train moving fifty miles an hour. Lima Slim was famous for the things he had done. Famous to bums anyway.

There was a bull at the Northampton yard named Arnold Choke some said was as bad as Lima Slim, which was why Killian didn't want to go there. After a long time of standing in the half-open doorway, he felt the train slowing down. Killian didn't know why, there wasn't a town ahead he could see. Maybe they were approaching a switch. He wondered if the train would come to a complete stop, but it didn't stop, and after a few seconds of losing speed, in a series of quick violent jerks, it began to accelerate again. Killian jumped. It wasn't really going that slow, and he hit hard on his left foot, and the gravel slid away under his heel. The foot twisted underneath him, and a sharp pain stabbed through his ankle. He did not shout when he pitched face first into the wet brush.

It was October or November maybe, Killian didn't know, and in the woods by the train tracks was a carpet of dead leaves in colors of rust and butter. Killian limped across them. The leaves were not all gone from the trees. Here and there was a flare of crimson, streaks of ember-orange. A cold white smoke lay low to the ground in among the trunks of the birch and the spruce. On a wet stump, Killian sat for a while and held his ankle gently in his hands, while the sun rose higher, and the morning mist burned away. His shoes were burst and held together by dirt-caked strips of burlap, and his toes were so cold they were almost numb. Gage had had better shoes, but Killian had left them, just as he left the blanket. He had tried to pray over Gage's body, but had not been able to remember any of the Bible, except a sentence that went *Mary kept all these things, pondering them in her heart,* and that was from the birth of Jesus and nothing to say over a dead man.

It would be a warm day, although when Killian at last stood it was still cool in under the shadows of the pines. He followed the tracks until his ankle was throbbing too badly to go on and he had to sit on the embankment and rest again. It was swelling badly now, and, when he put weight on it, he felt a bitter, electric pain shoot through the bone. He had always trusted Gage to know when to jump. He had trusted Gage to know everything.

There was a white cottage away through the trees. Killian only glanced at it, and looked back at his ankle, but then he lifted his head and looked into the trees again. On the trunk of a nearby pine, some-one had snapped away some bark and carved an X in the wood and rubbed coal in the X so it would stand out black. There were no secret hobo marks like some said, or if there were, Killian didn't know what they were and neither had Gage. An X like that, though, sometimes meant you could get something to eat at a place. Killian was strongly aware of the tight emptiness in his stomach.

He walked unsteadily through the trees to the yard behind the cottage and then hesitated at the edge of the woods. The paint was peeling and the windows were obscured by grime. Close against the back of the house was a garden bed, a long rectangle of earth with the rough dimensions of a grave. Nothing was growing in it.

Killian was standing there looking at the house when he noticed the girls. He had not seen them at first because they were so still and quiet. He had come at the cottage from the rear, but the forest extended up and around the side of the house, and the girls were there, kneeling in some ferns with their backs to him. He could not see what they were doing, but they were almost perfectly motionless. There were two of them, kneeling in their Sunday dresses. Each of them had white-blonde hair, long and brushed and clean, and each had in their hair an arrangement of little brassy combs.

He stood and watched them and they knelt and were very still. One of them turned her head and looked back at him. She had a heart-shaped face and her eyes were a glacial shade of blue. She regarded him with no expression. In another moment the other girl turned her head to look at him as well. This other smiling a little. The smiling one was possibly seven. Her expressionless sister was perhaps ten. He lifted his hand in greeting. The unsmiling girl watched him for a moment longer, then turned her head away. He could not see what she was kneeling in front of, but whatever it was held her interest completely. The younger girl did not wave either, but seemed to nod at him before she too went back to looking at whatever was on the ground before them. Their silence and stillness unsettled him.

He crossed the yard to the back door. The screen door was orange with rust, and bellied outwards, pulling free from the frame in places. He took off his hat and was going to climb the steps to knock, but the inner door opened first and a woman appeared behind the screen. Killian stopped with his hat in his hands and put his begging face on.

The woman could have been thirty or forty or fifty. Her face was so drawn it seemed almost starved and her lips were thin and colorless. A dishrag hung from the waist strap of her apron.

"Hello, ma'am," Killian said. "I'm hungry. I was wonderin' if I could have somethin' to eat. A bite of toast maybe."

"You haven't had any breakfast anywhere?"

"No ma'am."

"They give away a breakfast at Blessed Heart. Don't you know that?"

"Ma'am, I don't even know where that is."

She nodded briefly. "I'll make you toast. You can have eggs too if you want them. Do you want them?"

"Well. I guess if you made 'em, I wouldn't throw 'em in the road."

That was what Gage always said when he was offered more than he asked for, and it made the housewives laugh, but she didn't laugh, perhaps because he wasn't Gage and it didn't sound the same coming from him. Instead she only nodded once more and said, "All right. Scrape your feet on the—" she looked at his shoes and stopped speaking for a moment. "Look at those shoes. When you come in just take those shoes off and leave them by the door."

"Yes ma'am."

He looked again at the girls before he climbed the steps, but their backs were to him and they paid him no mind. He entered and removed his shoes and walked across the chilled linoleum in his dirty bare feet. There was an odd stinging sensation in his ankle every time he stepped on the left foot. By the time he sat there were already eggs sputtering in the pan.

"I know how you wound up at my back door. I know why you stopped at my house. Same reason all the other men stop here," she said, and he thought she was going to say something about the tree with the X on it, but she didn't. "It's because the train runs a little slower going into that switch, quarter a mile back, and all of you jump off so you won't have to see Arnold Choke in Northampton. Isn't that about it? Did you jump off at the switch?"

"Yes ma'am."

"Cause of Arnold Choke?"

"Yes ma'am. I've heard he's one you want to avoid."

"He's just got the reputation he does because of his last name. Arnold Choke isn't a danger to anyone. He's old and he's fat and if any of you ran from him he'd probably pass out trying to get you. Not that he'd ever run. He might run somewhere if he heard they were selling burgers two for a dime," she said. "You listen now. That train is going thirty miles an hour when it hits that switch. It doesn't slow hardly at all. Jumping off there is a lot more dangerous than going into the yard at Northampton."

"Yes ma'am," he said, and rubbed his left leg.

"There's a pregnant girl tried to get off there last year who jumped into a tree and broke her neck. Do you hear me?"

"Yes ma'am."

"A pregnant girl. Traveling with her husband. You ought to pass that around. Let other people know they're better off to stay on the train until she's good and stopped. Here's your eggs. You like some jam on this toast?"

"If it's no trouble ma'am. Thank you ma'am. I can't tell you how good this smells."

She leaned against the kitchen counter holding her spatula and watched him eat. He did not speak, but ate quickly, and in all that time she stared at him and said nothing.

"Well," she said when he was done. "I'll put a couple more in the pan for you."

"That's all right. This was plenty."

"You don't want them?"

He hesitated, unsure how to answer. It was a difficult question.

"He wants them," she said, and cracked two eggs into her pan.

"Do I look that hungry?"

"Hungry isn't the word. You got a look like a stray dog ready to knock over trashcans for something to eat."

When she set the plate in front of him he said, "If there's somethin' I can do to work this off, ma'am, I'd be glad to do it."

"Thank you. But there isn't anything."

"I wish you'd think of somethin'. I appreciate you openin' your kitchen to me this way. I'm not a no-account. I don't have no fear to work."

"Where are you from?"

"Missouri."

"I thought you were southern. You got a funny way of sounding. Where are you going to?"

"I don't know," he said.

She didn't ask him anything else, and stood against the counter with her spatula and again watched him eat. Then she went out and left him by himself in the kitchen.

When he was finished, he sat at the table unsure of what to do, or if he should go. While he was trying to decide, she came back, holding a pair of low black boots in one hand, a pair of black socks in the other.

"Put these on and see if they fit," she said.

"No ma'am. I can't."

"You can and you will. Put them on. Your feet look about the right size for them."

He put on the socks and pulled the boots on over them. He was tender about sliding his left foot in, but still there was a sharp stab of pain through the ankle. He sucked in a harsh breath.

"Is there something wrong with that foot?" she asked.

"I twisted it."

"Getting off that train at the switch?"

"Yes ma'am."

She shook her head at him. "Others will die. All for fear of a fat old man with six teeth in his head."

The boots were a little loose, perhaps a size too big. A zipper ran up the inside of each boot. The leather was black and clean and only a little scuffed at the tips. They looked as if they had hardly been worn.

"How do they fit you?"

"Good. I can't have them though. These are just new."

"Well. They aren't doing me any good and my husband doesn't need them. He died in July."

"I'm sorry."

"So am I," she said with no change in her face. "Would you like some coffee? I didn't offer you coffee."

He did not answer so she poured him a cup, and herself a cup, and she sat down at the table.

"He died in a truck accident," she said. "It was a WPA truck. It rolled over. He wasn't the only one who died. Five other men were killed with him. Maybe you read about it. It was in lots of papers."

He didn't reply. He hadn't heard of it.

"He was driving—my husband. Some say it was his fault, that he was careless at the wheel. They investigated it. I guess maybe it was his fault." She was quiet for a while and then said, "The only good thing about his death is he doesn't have to walk around with that guilt on him. Living with having it his fault. That would have spoiled him inside."

Killian wished he was Gage. Gage would have known what to say. Gage would have reached across the table then and touched her hand. Killian sat in the dead man's boots and struggled for something. At last he blurted: "The most terrible things happen to the best people. The kindest people. Most of the time it isn't for any reason at all. It's just stupid luck. If you don't know for sure it was his fault, why make yourself feel sick thinkin' it was? It's hard enough just to lose someone that means something to you, without all that."

"Well. I try not to think about it," she said. "I do miss him. But I thank God every night for the twelve years we got to have together. I thank God for his daughters. I see his eyes in theirs."

"Yes," he said.

"They don't know what to do. They've never been so confused."

"Yes," he said.

They sat at the table for a little while, and then the woman said, "You look about his size all around. I can let you have one of his shirts and a pair of trousers as well as the boots."

"No ma'am. I wouldn't feel right. Takin' things from you I can't pay for."

"Stop that now. We won't talk about pay. I look for every small bit of good that can come out of such a bad thing. I'd like to give them to you. That would make me feel better," she said and smiled. He had took her hair for gray, wrapped up in a bun behind her head, but where she sat now she was in some watery sunlight from one of the windows, and he saw for the first time that her hair was blonde-white just like her daughters'.

She got up and went out again. While she was away, he cleaned the dishes. The woman returned in a short time with a pair of khaki trousers and suspenders, a heavy plaid shirt, and undershirt. She directed him to a back bedroom off the kitchen, and left him while he dressed. The shirt was big and loose and had a faint male smell on it, not disagreeable—also a pipe smoke smell. Killian had seen a corncob pipe on the mantle over the stove.

He came out with his dirty and ripped clothes under his arm, feeling clean and fresh and ordinary, a pleasant fullness in his stomach. She sat at the table holding one of his old shoes. She was smiling faintly, and peeling off the mud-caked wrap of burlap around it.

"Them shoes have earned their rest," Killian said. "I'm almost ashamed of the way I've treated 'em."

She lifted her head and contemplated him quietly. Looked at his trousers. He had rolled the trouser cuffs up over his ankles.

"I wasn't sure if he was your size or not," she said. "I thought he was bigger, but I didn't know. I thought it might only be my memory making him bigger."

"Well. He was just as big as you recall."

"He gets to seeming bigger," she said. "The further I get away from him."

There was nothing he could do for her to pay back what he owed for the clothes and the food. She told him Northampton was three miles and he ought to go now, because he would probably be hungry again by the time he got there, and there was a lunch at the Blessed Heart of the Virgin Mary where he could get a bowl of beans and a slice of bread. She told him there was a Hooverville on the east side of the Connecticut River, but if he went she advised him not to stay long because it was often raided and men were frequently arrested for squatting. At the door, she said it was better to get arrested at the trainyard than to try to jump off early of the yard on a freight that was going too fast. She said she didn't want him to jump off any more trains, except ones that were stopped, or just inching along; it might be worse than a twisted ankle next time. He nodded and asked again if there was anything he could do for her. She said she had just told him something he could do for her.

He wanted to take her hand. Gage would have taken her hand and promised to pray for her and the husband she had lost. He wished he could tell her about Gage. Killian found, though, that he could not reach to touch her hand, or lift his arms in any way, and he didn't trust his voice to speak. He was often crushed by the decency of other people who had almost nothing themselves; at times he felt their kindnesses so powerfully he thought it would destroy some delicate inner part of him.

As he was crossing the yard to the road, in his new outfit, he glanced into the trees and saw the two girls in among the ferns. They were standing now, and each of them held a bouquet of wilty looking old flowers, and they were staring at the ground. He stopped and watched them, wondering what they were doing, what was on the ground beyond the ferns that he couldn't see. As he stood there, both turned their heads—first the oldest girl, and then her younger sister, just as before—and looked back at him.

Killian smiled uncertainly and walked, limping, across the yard to them. He waded through the dew damp ferns to stand behind them. Just past where the girls stood was a patch of cleared ground, and on the ground a piece of black sacking. On the sack lay a third girl, the youngest yet, in a white dress with lace stitching at the collar and sleeves. Her bone-china white hands were folded across her breastbone, and a small bouquet was beneath them. Her eyes were closed. The muscles in her face trembled as she struggled not to smile. She was no more than five. A wreath of dried daisies around her blonde hair. A heap of dead wilted flowers at her feet. A Bible opened at her side.

"Our sister Kate is dead," said the oldest girl.

"This is where we're having the wake," said the middle daughter.

Kate lay very still on top the sacking. Her eyes remained shut, but she had to bite her lips not to grin.

"Do you want to play?" asked the middle daughter. "Do you want to play the game? You could lay down. You could be the dead person and we could cover you with flowers and read out of the Bible and sing *Nearer My God To Thee*."

"I'll cry," said the oldest girl. "I can make myself cry whenever I want."

Killian stood there. He looked at the girl on the ground and then at the two mourners. He said at last, "I don't believe this is my kind of game. I don't want to be the dead person."

The oldest girl flicked her gaze across him, then stared into his face.

"Why not?" she asked. "You're dressed the part."

Pond on Morris Road

Don Thompson

This morning, cold and overcast,
wind without letup,
I can hear the dying tule reeds
rub against each other.
Maybe I'm listening to their last words:
hoarse, like worn-out sandpaper
putting the final touches
on silence.

"No. You listen to me, Dad."

Joe Ballard

We were happy together. Prosperous. But you missed it all, in bed with her. I'm reminded how hollow you are when I see female stockings on the stairs, summer dress on the roof,

after viewing city lights, draped over the sapling mom is buried under. To cover your shame. And one night when that intern's back is arched and yours is straightened, that

sapling will grow, fed by ashes, push its roots into the joists of you, woody vines, twist around electrical wires, sever insulation, remove your power. And she will bloom

through the sheetrock of you, splintering that stud that makes you stand proud, mangling crown molding, sill severing, blunt force shower head, back splash countertop.

The roots. Will grow—the size of breasts before the cancer is taken out—when you started looking at other ones—and will burst into the walls of you, deck the halls and into the

floors of you, out the windows and through the mind of you—bringing you down to the basement, where is *all that is left* of you.

My Name is Benjamin Wilkes—15,111!!!

Tyler Wilborn

I. Last night I did too much of the word games that Mom hates where I count the number of letters she speaks in a sentence and then yell it out as fast as I can after her sentence is over—153! She talked at me in her screaming voice so I hid with my favorite book called *Numbers, Letters and Signs: A Study of Trigonometric Forms*—118! I recited the first page of the book which is called "equations—a beginner's guide," and then sang Happy Birthday to everyone whose birthday it was that day which was four people I knew and six people which I had learned from the website last month in computer class with Miss Nancy—228 (most!!)! This list included my aunt Beth and my second cousin Joe from San Antonio and his boyfriend Kenny from Massachusetts and my sister Megan who is at school in another city that is 345.7 miles away—159! Tomorrow it will be seven more people's birthdays but only people I see at school which is Tualatin Middle School and the office lady Carrie who always lets me call my mom when I get in trouble doing word games which I only do if I get nervous but also sometimes if I don't know what to say—215!

II. *There is no one here by that name.* The notice stamped on the front of the envelope marked "return to sender: Brenda Matrice 4359 Lehman Street, Tualatin, OR" formed a curious block letter font that superimposed itself over the neatly written cursive that had adorned thousands of envelopes in years past. She tossed it blithely to the side, her eyes falling to the growing pile of envelopes stamped with the very same block letter font indicating that, in fact, whoever they thought she was sending these letters to no longer existed.

She wasn't upset; well, she was, but, she thought, it just would have been nice to be informed if she had moved and, if she had moved, to where she had moved so there could be no more of this confusing block letter font and forty-six (forty-seven, now) letters marked "return to sender" sitting in a pile on her desk.

She sat down quickly, the phrase *there is no one here by that name* repeating over in her head. She pulled out an envelope and wrote the same address for the forty-eighth time. *There is no one here by that name.* What was that about? Who had said that? She waded through the fog of her thoughts. A relative, she thought. Or the boy she saw every week at the grocery store. That was it. She had asked about the Gala apples, which were her favorite, and he had said "there are none here by that name."

She continued writing the address, neatly scrawling the name "Jane Maxwell" above the numbers. She stamped the envelope, sealed it, and set it in a pile to her left labeled "to-do." Shakily, she stood and crossed the living room into the foyer. She grabbed her keys and left, wearing her blue sweater, backwards, like she always did of late, and her slippers. Her nightgown brushed the tops of her feet as she stepped out the door.

III. Yesterday I saw the same lady I always see when we go the store on Sundays for exactly 37 minutes (it takes us 9 minutes and 47 seconds to get there usually but sometimes 10 minutes and 26 seconds if we have to stop at the stop light that is .635 miles away from our driveway—last Christmas Mom gave me a step counter which counts your steps and also a GPS which measures the distance to and from anywhere we go)—328! The lady is old and wears a blue sweater and when I see her she always has four things in her cart which are a can of tuna and a green sponge labeled *Everbrite!* and one box of twelve square crackers and one small jar which I can't tell what it is except it has a small fish on it—220! Sometimes the lady looks at me and smiles and shows 7 teeth which are yellow—78! When she smiles I scream 7!!! which makes Mom talk at me in her screaming voice in public which makes me want to hide with my favorite book called *Numbers, Letters, and Signs: A Study of Trigonometric Forms* but I can't because we are at the store so usually I start to have tears and shout the numbers of all the things in the store which is 237 cereal boxes and 112 bags of chips until Mom takes me out of the store to go home and be well—371 (most!!)!

IV. She shook the cold off her thinly covered shoulders as she stepped inside her front door. Her watch read two o'clock, almost exactly four hours after she'd left. Must be wrong, she thought, as she hobbled into her living room. A fish tank dominated the center of the small space. She smiled slyly, and pulled the fish food out of her shopping bag.

"Hello, Little Ones." She sprinkled some flakes into the water and watched, eyes sparkling, as her three fish pecked for scraps. "There you go." She dropped the food into the basket underneath the tank where a dozen half-empty bottles lay. She smiled again and sat down on the faded maroon sofa that faced the fish tank. She had received the tank as a gift from a girl a few years ago. The girl was middle-aged, but looked young, and had three kids who helped haul it in. She could picture the girl almost perfectly, like she'd seen her somewhere before, but couldn't quite remember. The smile returned as she let her eyelids take over her foggy thoughts and drifted off to sleep.

V. Today Mom had one of her sicks which always means I get to have an extra hour of reading from my favorite book which is called *Numbers, Letters, and Signs: A Study of Trigonometric Forms* before I go to bed—166! I am almost all memorized through chapter 2 which is called "further trigonometric study" and which has 13 equations in it—106! Sometimes I sit and try to solve the equations with the numbers I counted that day and I mostly always end up with the same problems because I always count the same things which is the backpacks at school and the birthdays of my most favorite helper Mr. Kris from school and my home helper Miss Claire—264 (most!!)!

VI. She awoke to the twitch of her muscles; she looked around her living room, her heart pounding in her chest. Where was he? Why hadn't he come home from work? Why hadn't he at least called? She remembered his face like she'd seen him just that morning. The picture of him, the two of them, blared lucid in her mind like every memory of them now suddenly did. She shuffled to her room and silently pulled out the scrapbook from under her bed, caressing the cover, then feeling her way along the edges of each picture. She remembered him so well now—his touch as he pressed his fingers into her shoulders, lifting her chin just to look at her. His eyes decorated her mind with a thousand paint drops; a rainbow of moments that streamed like a real-time movie, and, for now, she could watch and savor every sweet memory. The way he whispered the very words she thought she'd never hear and looked at her like she was the only person his whole world knew; the way he colored her cheeks with a single brush of his lips against hers. The way he colored her world every day until their very last one. She watched as the pages flew by, each one pricking her quiet memory awake for just another moment. Her tears smeared the pictures until she no longer knew what she was crying about. Until his face became blurry, and the movie stopped playing, and the clarity of her tears slipped into the fog, seeping over her mind with mysterious warmth as she fell asleep once more.

VII. It is my favorite day of the week which is Wednesday because that is the day that Mom works at her other place which means that after school I get to watch my favorite movie which is *The Lady and the Tramp* which is my favorite because I get to count each animal in the movie which is 37 and shout the number of animals in each part which is usually between 3 and 26 but is sometimes 31—313 (most!!)! While Mom works my home helper Miss Claire watches the movie with me and then takes me to the park after which only happens when it is nice outside which means it is above 62 degrees Fahrenheit—294! I like these days because it means we don't do special time which is when Miss Claire hugs me and rubs me and I feel weird which she tells me is normal and that I don't need to tell my mom since it is just because we're friends—183! But since today it is 64 degrees Fahrenheit I would get to go to the park where I can swing and shout my equations while Miss Claire reads them to me from *Numbers, Letters, and Signs: A Study of Trigonometric Forms*—165!

VIII. Her eyelids raised reluctantly to face the light coming into the room as her mind lifted itself out of the haze of her troubled sleep. She navigated the same fog that came with every morning and surveyed her bleak surroundings, becoming aware of a tissue still crumpled in her left hand. The unfamiliar room pressed upon her a sense of familiar urgency—like someone was watching her every move. At her side lay an open book of pictures; some of her, some of a man she did not know, and some of them together. His smile haunted her. She shook her head, closed the book, and stood up. She wandered across the room and opened the top drawer of the antique dresser, which stood at the foot of the bed. She traced her finger along the familiar groove just above the drawer, smiling at its constant presence. As if in a dream, she knew what to do—she knew the routine of this place—and this room, this house—but nothing else about it.

IX. Today at school I did too much of the word games and got sent to Mrs. Carrie in the office whose birthday is November 2, 1961 and who always calls my mom when I have trouble and lets me talk to Mr. Kris whose birthday is October 16, 1968 and is my favorite helper because he always lets me drink whatever soda I want which is usually grape from the fridge in his office which I get when I do well—316! When Mrs. Carrie was off the phone she said my mom couldn't get me so my home helper Miss Claire was coming but I got nervous because it was only 58.3 degrees outside which meant that we wouldn't go to the park which meant that Miss Claire would want to have special time so I started doing word games again in a loud voice like a speaker which made Mr. Kris ask why I did them so loud and I told him it was because my mom couldn't get me and Miss Claire had to which meant that we wouldn't go to the park because it was less than 62 degrees and that she would want to have special time—463 (most!!)! Since Mr. Kris didn't know what special time was I told him it was when Miss Claire hugged me and put her hand on my privates and sometimes took my hand and put it on her private parts which made me feel weird but which she said was normal because we were friends and not to tell my mom—228! After I told Mr. Kris about special time I got shaky like I do when I'm nervous and had to lay down and couldn't even practice my equations—112! After I lay down Mr. Kris helped me sit up and let me practice my equations and drink whatever soda I wanted which was grape which he got me from the special fridge for teachers in the back of his office while he called my mom—181! I still did my word games but since Mr. Kris said it was very good that I told him about special time and that Miss Claire wouldn't come get me I didn't feel shaky and instead I could count the equations which I had memorized which was 32 from my favorite book which is called *Numbers, Letters, and Signs: A Study of Trigonometric Forms*—293!

X. She scattered the pile of letters across her already disheveled table, the memory of her maze-like house surfacing amid her confused reality. They all read the same name: "Jane Maxwell," but there was something puzzling to her about the way they were written. She remembered the name, scrawled somewhere in a book with pictures; pictures she'd seen before but didn't know. Drearily, she sorted through them; each one, save the most recent, reading *there is no one here by that name*. She picked up the newest one, determined to send it—determined to figure out the meaning behind the unfamiliar words.

XI. Yesterday after I told Mr. Kris about special time Mom came with two police with shiny buttons who asked me about Miss Claire and I started to get shaky even though Mr. Kris patted my arm and said it was good that they were there because Miss Claire was in trouble even though she said she was my friend—247! I told the police about special time and Miss Claire and how she would always want to have it if it was less than 62 degrees outside and that it made me feel weird but she said we were just friends—158! Then the police people said thank you and sorry and gave me a sticker that looked like their buttons which I put on the back of my hand so I could see it—116! When Mom took me home she had tears which made me feel the feeling of tears without having them and when I asked her why she was crying she said it was because she was mad at Miss Claire—160! I said it was okay because Miss Claire said we were friends but Mom said that Miss Claire and I weren't friends and that I wouldn't be seeing her anymore so I got shaky and started playing word games and practicing my equations but only in my head because I know she hates them and I didn't want her to have any more tears—274! On the way home she got me my favorite ice cream from the chocolate store which is Rocky Road which I love because I get to pick the marshmallows out and count how many there are which was 26—147!

XII. Fish food. That was what she needed. Fish food and something to clean the tank. Her mind was instilled with urgency as she wandered out the door, mysterious letter in hand, towards her near-ancient grey Camry, which sat in the drizzling rain. It sputtered as she drove her usual Sunday route to the grocery store. Fish food. And a sponge. For what? For her fish. A sponge. A sponge and...a fish? The clear list in her head slowly lost itself within the fog—the immense, suffocating fog that unrelentingly covered her mind. She squinted her eyes, both to remember and to see through the steam-covered windows. She blinked back frustrated tears. There was too much. Too much to think of. Too much to wade through. Too much to squint at; and then there was him. Standing, smiling, in his polo shirt and plaid shorts, his round glasses sitting low on his nose as they did when he was smiling wide, showing the teeth that had always been a little bit crooked. It was sunny; he was in the doorway to their bedroom, illuminated by the light coming in the window, waiting with his hand extended as if reaching for hers. He kept reaching, mouthing something, and smiling. She remembered. It was Sunday: time for church. Time for them to walk hand in hand out the door. On the way, they would talk; about each other, about the night before, about their kids, their grandkids, their church, how happy they were, and he would say "I love you," and she would smile and pat his leg—as predictable as the groove on her dresser—and ask what they needed from the grocery store because she would go later.

But it was too late to remember. It was too late to try to bring him back to life. It was too late, as his face slipped back into the merciless fog, to swerve out of the other lane.

XIII. Today I woke up in a room which was white and had exactly 3 chairs which were red and dark pink and brown and which also had 7 roses on each one and notes with my name on them—137! When I woke up I got shaky like I do when I'm nervous because I remembered that Mom and I had gotten hurt in the car and I didn't know where she was so I started playing the word games really loud with the things around me which was 3 chairs and 21 roses and 7 notes which all said "Benjamin" and "Get well soon" and 29 buttons on the machine next to my bed—256! While I was counting there was one person in a white coat who came in who said her name was Delia and that she was there to help me which was good because I started to get shaky again when I woke up because I wasn't sure how I woke up in the white room or why everything hurt so bad—204! After that I started to play word games and asked for my favorite book which is called *Numbers, Letters, and Signs: A Study of Trigonometric Forms* which they gave to me but it was ripped from the car crash they said so it was hard to memorize any more equations—203! Then Mr. Kris came in and I got to tell him all the things I remembered about the accident which was that I was practicing my equations and we were heading to the grocery store because it was Sunday which is when we always go for exactly 37 minutes (it takes us 9 minutes and 47 seconds to get there usually but sometimes 10 minutes and 26 seconds if we have to stop at the stop light that is .635 miles away from our driveway)—341! But we never got to the store because another car hit us and my mom yelled my name louder than I've ever played any word games and then I woke up in the white room and I didn't know how I woke up there—162! After that Mr. Kris asked me if I knew what had happened to the car that hit us and he showed me a picture of the lady I see in the blue sweater at the store every Sunday who has four things in her cart and he said she went to a better place which I said was good because that's where old people have to go which is what my mom said about Grammie when she stopped coming over every Monday for exactly 103 minutes which is one hour and 43 minutes—353 (most!!)! Then Mr. Kris said he had to say something about my mom which was that she was with Gram-mie which made me feel shaky like I do when I'm nervous and do word games really loud because I didn't know what to do—164! I counted every freckle on Mr. Kris's face which was 42 and a mole which looked like a freckle but it wasn't so I didn't count it and then I asked when my mom would be back and then Mr. Kris got tears which made me feel like I should have tears and he said that Mom died and that's what he meant when he said she was with Grammie which made me have tears that made it hard to breathe so I couldn't even play word games which Mr. Kris said was okay—352! When I could breathe again I tried to practice my equations from my favorite book which is called

Numbers, Letters, and Signs: A Study of Trigonometric Forms and since I couldn't remember I ripped out 5 pages and played word games so loud until I was too shaky to play anymore because I didn't know what to do—252! Then Mr. Kris had tears and so did Delia which made me feel like I had tears even though I didn't because I was sad so I did more word games and practiced my equations from my favorite book which is called *Numbers, Letters, and Signs: A Study of Trigonometric Forms* and which my mom gave to me exactly 13 days ago which was exactly 11 days before she left—286!

Childhood at Home

Sunni Brown Wilkinson

Burkwood against brick, and the tendrils
of the bean plants curl like tiny pigs' tails.

Mother is crying again deep in the house.
The burkwood is a white flower

that blooms in spring and smells
like the bottom of dreams, and inside a room

that pavane endlessly plays.
Father's postal hat on the railing says

he's there, comforting her, and outside
the bean plants reach in the dirt and the light

muscles through apertures of cloud
and the clouds are not so much scarves

as horses, all the horses you ever wanted,
riding the sky and calling deep in their throats.

You can ride them into tomorrow, you with the blue
veins that branch through you like bean plants

just under the skin, the ragged white flowers
of your hands against the brick of a house

where a door inside opens and closes
like a throat opens and closes

like a cry that becomes a song
only you hear and understand.

Sump and Tule Reeds, Morris Road

Don Thompson

Sparrows have everything in common:
same song, same ancestral mannerisms
unchanged forever, nests
like entry-level tract houses,
and their colors identical
as if God got a deal
on unlimited gallons of paint
so drab no one would buy it.
Nevertheless, each sparrow puffs up
with its own life
that it shares with no other—
brief and anonymous,
but irreplaceable.

Kansas

first published in *Volume II, Issue II*

Stephen Dobyns

The boy hitchhiking on the back-country Kansas road was nineteen-years-old. He had been dropped there by a farmer in a Model T Ford who had turned off to the north. Then he waited for three hours. It was July and there were no clouds. The wheat fields were flat and went straight to the horizon. The boy had two plums and he ate them. A blue Plymouth coupe went by with a man and a woman. They were laughing. The woman had blond hair and it was all loose and blew from the window. They didn't even see the boy. The strands of straw-colored hair seemed to be waving to him. Half an hour later a farmer stopped in a Ford pickup covered with a layer of dust. The boy clambered into the front seat. The farmer took off again without glancing at him. A forty-five revolver lay next to the farmer's buttocks on the seat. Seeing it, the boy felt something electric go off inside of him. The revolver was old and there were rust spots on the barrel. Black electrician's tape was wrapped around the handle.

"You seen a woman and a man go by here in a Plymouth coupe?" asked the farmer. He pronounced it "koo-pay."

The boy said he had.

"How long ago?"

"About thirty minutes."

The farmer had light blue eyes and there was stubble on his chin. Perhaps he was forty, but to the boy he looked old. His skin was leather-colored from the sun. The farmer pressed his foot to the floor and the pickup roared. It was a dirt road and the boy had to hold his hands against the dashboard to keep from being bounced around. It was hot and both windows were open. There was grit in the boy's eyes and on his tongue. He kept glancing sideways at the revolver.

"They friends of yours?" asked the boy.

The farmer didn't look at him. "That's my wife," he said. "I'm going to put a bullet in her head." He put a hand to the revolver to make sure it was still there. "The man too," he added.

The boy didn't say anything. He was hitchhiking back to summer school from Oklahoma. He was the middle of three boys and the only one who had left home. He had already spent a year at the University of Oklahoma and was spending the summer at Lawrence. And there were other places, farther places. The boy played the piano. He intended to go to those farther places.

"What did they do?" the boy asked at last.

"You just guess," said the farmer.

The pickup was going about fifty miles per hour. The boy was afraid of seeing the dust cloud from the Plymouth up ahead, but there was only straight road. Then he was afraid that the Plymouth might have pulled off someplace. He touched his tongue to his upper lip but it was just one dry thing against another. Getting into the pickup, the boy had had a clear idea of the direction of his life. He meant to go to New York City at the end of summer. He meant to play the piano in Carnegie Hall. The farmer and his forty-five seemed to stand between him and that future. They formed a wall that the boy was afraid to climb over.

"Do you have to kill them?" the boy asked. He didn't want to talk but he felt unable to remain silent.

The farmer had a red boil on the side of his neck and he kept touching it with two fingers. "When you have something wicked, what do you do?" asked the farmer.

The boy wanted to say he didn't know or he wanted to say he would call the police, but the farmer would have no patience with those answers. And the boy also wanted to say he would forgive the wickedness, but he was afraid of that answer as well. He was afraid of making the farmer angry and so he only shrugged.

"You stomp it out," said the farmer. "That's what you do—you stomp it out."

The boy stared straight ahead, searching for the dust cloud and hoping not to see it. The hot air seemed to bend in front of them. The boy was so frightened of seeing the dust cloud that he was sure he saw it. A little puff of gray getting closer. The pickup went straight down the middle of the road. There was no other traffic. Even if there had been other cars, the boy felt certain that the farmer wouldn't have moved out of the way. The wheat on either side of the road was coated with layers of dust, making it a reddish color, the color of dried blood.

"What about the police?" asked the boy.

"It's my wife," said the farmer. "It's my problem."

The boy never did see the dust cloud. They reached Lawrence and the boy got out as soon as he could. His shirt was stuck to his back and he kept rubbing his palms on his dungarees. He thanked the farmer but the man didn't look at him, he just kept staring straight ahead

"Don't tell the police," said the farmer. His hand rested lightly on the forty-five beside him on the seat.

"No," said the boy. "I promise." He slammed shut the dusty door of the pickup.

The boy didn't tell the police. For several days he didn't tell anyone at all. He looked at the newspapers twice a day for news of a killing, but he didn't find anything. More than the farmer's gun, he had been frightened by the strength of the farmer's resolve. It had been like a chunk of stone and compared to it the boy had felt as soft as a piece of white bread. The boy never knew what happened. Perhaps nothing had happened.

The summer wound to its conclusion. The boy went to New York. He never did play in Carnegie Hall. His piano playing never got good enough. The war came and went. He wasn't a boy any longer. He was a married man with two sons. The family moved to Michigan. The man was a teacher, then a minister. His own parents died. He told his sons the story about the farmer in the pickup. "What do you think happened?" they asked. Nobody knew. Perhaps the farmer caught up with them; perhaps he didn't. The man's sons went off to college and began their own lives. The man and his wife moved to New Hampshire. They grew old. Sixty years went by between that summer in Kansas and the present. The man entered his last illness. He stayed at home but he couldn't get out of bed. His wife gave him shots of morphine. He began to have dreams even when he was awake. The visiting nurse was always chipper. "Feeling better today?" she would ask. He tried to be polite, but he had no illusions. He went from one shot a day to two, and then three. The doctor said, "Give him as many as he needs." His wife started to ask about the danger of addiction, then she said nothing.

The man hardly knew when he was asleep or awake. He hardly knew if one day had passed or many. He had oxygen. He didn't eat. The space between his eyes and the bedroom wall was always occupied with people of his invention, people of his past. He would lift his hand to wave them away, only to find his hand still lying motionless on the counterpane. Even music distracted him now. Always he was listening for something in the distance.

The boy was standing by the side of a dirt road. A Ford pickup stopped beside him and he got in. The farmer lifted a forty-five revolver. "I'm going to shoot my wife in the head."

"No," said the boy, "don't do it!"

The farmer drove fast. He had a red boil on the side of his neck and he kept touching it with two fingers. They found the Plymouth coupe pulled off into a hollow. There were shade trees and a brook. The farmer jammed down the brakes and the pickup slid sideways across the dirt. The man and woman were in the front seat of the Plymouth. Their clothes were half off. They jumped out of the car. The woman had big red breasts. The farmer jumped out with his forty-five. "No!" shouted the boy. The farmer shot the man in the head. His whole head exploded and he fell down in the dust. His head was just a broken thing on the ground. The woman covered her face and tried to cover her breasts as well. The farmer shot her as well. Bits of dust floated on the surface of her blood. "One last for me," said the farmer. He put the barrel of the gun in his mouth. "No, no!" cried the boy.

The boy was standing by the side of a dirt road. A Ford pickup stopped beside him and he got in. "I'm going to shoot my wife," said the farmer. He had a big revolver on the seat beside him.

"You can't" said the boy.

They talked all the way to Lawrence. The farmer was crying. "I've always been good to her," he said. He had a red boil on the side of his neck and he kept touching it.

"Give the gun to the police," said the boy.

"I'm afraid," said the farmer.

"You needn't be," said the boy. "The police won't hurt you."

They drove to the police station. The boy told the desk sergeant what had happened. The sergeant shook his head. He took the revolver away from the farmer. "We'll get her back, sir," he said. "Wife stealing's not permitted around here."

"I could have got in real trouble," said the farmer.

The boy was standing by the side of a dirt road. A pickup stopped beside him and he got in. The farmer said, "I'm going to kill my wife."

The boy was too frightened to say anything. He kept looking at the forty-five revolver. He was sure that he would be shot himself. He regretted not staying in Oklahoma, where he had friends and family. He couldn't imagine why he had moved away. The farmer drove straight to Lawrence. The boy was bounced all over the cab of the pickup but he didn't say anything. He was afraid that something would happen to his hands and he wouldn't be able to play the piano. It seemed to him that playing the piano was the only important thing in the entire world. The farmer had a red boil on the side of his neck and he kept touching it.

When they got to Lawrence, the boy jumped out of the pickup and ran. He saw a policeman and told him what had happened. An hour later he was getting a hamburger at a White Tower restaurant. He heard shooting. He ran out and saw the farmer's dusty pickup. There were police cars with their lights flashing. The boy pushed through the crowd. The farmer was hanging half out of the door of his pickup truck. There was blood all over the front of his workshirt. The forty-five revolver lay on the pavement. The policemen were clapping each other on the back. They had big grins. The boy began cracking his knuckles. They made snapping noises.

The boy was standing by the side of a dirt road. A pickup stopped beside him and he got in. The farmer pointed a forty-five revolver at his head. "Get in here," he said. They drove toward Lawrence.

"I'm going to shoot my wife for wickedness," said the farmer.

"No," said the boy, "you must forgive her."

"I'm going to kill her," said the farmer, "and her fancy man besides."

The boy said, "You can't take the law into your own hands."

The farmer raised his forty-five revolver. "They're as good as dead." He had a red boil on the side of his neck.

The boy was a college student. It was the Depression. He wanted to go to New York and become a classical pianist. He had already been accepted by Juilliard. "Justice does not belong to you," said the boy.

"Wickedness must be punished," said the farmer.

They argued all the way to Lawrence. The boy stayed with the farmer. He could have jumped out of the pickup, but he didn't. The boy kept trying to convince him that he was wrong. The farmer drove to the train station.

The farmer's wife was in the waiting room with the man who had been driving the Plymouth coupe. She was very pretty, with blond hair and milky pink skin. She screamed when she saw the farmer. Her companion put his arms around her to protect her.

The boy hurried to stand between the woman and her husband. "Think of what you are doing," he said. "Think how you are throwing your life away." The first bullet struck him in the shoulder and whipped him around. He could see the woman open her mouth in a startled *Oh* of surprise. The second bullet caught him in the small of his back.

The man's family was with him in New Hampshire when he died: his wife and his two sons, neither of them young anymore. It was early evening in October at the very height of color. Even after sundown the maple trees seemed bright. The older son watched his father breathing. He kept twisting and trying to kick his feet. His face was very thin, his whole body was just a ridge under the middle of the sheet. He didn't talk anymore. He didn't want anyone to touch him. He seemed to be focusing his attention. He took a breath and they waited. He exhaled slowly. They continued to wait. He didn't breathe again. They waited several minutes. Then his wife removed the oxygen tubes from his nose, doing it quickly, as if afraid of doing something wrong.

The older son went back into the bedroom with the two men from the funeral home. They had a collapsible stretcher which they put next to the bed. They unrolled a dark blue body bag. They shifted the dead man onto the stretcher and wrestled him into the body bag, one at his feet, one at his head. The son stood in the doorway. The men from the funeral home muttered directions to each other. They were breathing heavily and their hair was mussed. At last they got him into the body bag. The son watched closely as the zipper was drawn up and across his father's face. It was a large silver zipper and the son watched it being pulled across his father's forehead. All the days after that he kept seeing its glittering progress, a picture repeating itself in his mind.

One Chance

Paulann Petersen

—*after filling out a* Teacher Assessment
of Suitability for Army Special Schools
*for Tony Herrara and dropping it
into the mail slot*

The form had asked me to please rate,
on a scale of 1 to 5, the applicant's
MENTAL STABILITY.
GENERAL HEALTH.
RESPECT FOR AUTHORITY.
                              He called me
Sweetpea once, his words surprising himself
more than anyone else. Everybody in class
laughed, especially me. Tony was pleased,
smiling slowly, his tongue tasting
the sour metal of new braces.
HONESTY.
DEPENDABILITY.
ABILITY TO LIVE IN CLOSE
PROXIMITY TO OTHERS.
                              When I stepped
between Monte and James, Tony stepped too,

barely touching Monte's arm, talking fast
to Monte about suspension, getting grounded,
cooling off, while I was talking
James out the door.
DILIGENCE.
POTENTIAL FOR LEADERSHIP.
INITIATIVE.
      A shepherd-mix wandered
into class during finals, one blue eye,
one brown. Tony borrowed my mug
for a water bowl, and although others
coaxed and whistled, it chose
to sleep by his desk. When the dog
grew restless, Tony lifted it in his arms,
carried it the length of the hall
before setting it down
on the grass outside.
      Tony's Assessment Form
on its way to the Army, I suddenly recalled
another boy, Jeremy, back at school one day,
discharged early after a scrape with a sergeant,
his hunger for action as persistent
as the florid tattoo on his arm.
Hair shorn, fatigues blade-creased,
Jeremy had pulled a desk up to mine to talk,
believing I was—besides himself—
the only one in that classroom
who wasn't a child.
"Got trained to run a million dollar

laser weapon. For tanks. I can hit one
a mile away. Zap a hole in it
just an inch wide. Heats up
what's inside to 5,000 degrees.
Sucks everything through
the hole out the back. Boom.
It's done. But tanks cost
big bucks. They only let me try it
on one."

    I wanted Tony's form back
from the Army, so I could tell
one other truth. Just one.
Yes, Antonio Herrara wants to be
among those few you'll choose,
wants the chance to wear
your special uniform. But what
you hope I'll praise in Tony
will make him
           unfit to serve.

Vapor

Warren Slesinger

Vapor (vay.por) n-s 1. Something
in the air: a mixture of suspended matter
that makes it difficult to see down a street
in Baghdad. 2. A mist with a man in it.

Vaporize (vay.por.ize) v. 1. Only
to convert into a vapor with the heat
of a high explosive. 2. To detonate
a mess of manhood high-strung on hate.

Vaporous (vay.por.us) adj. 1. What
is collecting in a cloud of Middle-Eastern
malice. 2. Rising from a blast of body
parts on the same old ground.

What People Do

Joe Ballard

You walk down the street in military uniform, going for coffee—
that's what everyone else does—a girl in blue stops you, *Thank you for
your service*, she smiles. When someone

is grateful you think of the first man you had to kill. A cemetery, you're
interlocked with the enemy. An electric urge surges into your chest,
and you push him. His head splashes

against bricks, body twists, femur erupts from his pocket. He collapses
down catacomb steps, and into darkness. But you don't tell her that.
I've had family in the military, she nods.

I understand the evils you've seen. Evils? Memory drowns into a
desert city, to a soccer field. Kids play a match, no shoes, fluorescent
shorts, full of laughter. The ball is paper-mache,

dyed into mazes of purples and golds, kicked between two rocks, scor-
ing a goal. The sun screams a little brighter, when the future pulls to a
stop. Two insurgents get out and bury

a bomb. And you step up. This is your job: to radio an airstrike on enemy fighters. This is your moment to make a difference in a war indifferent to life—and you call it in. The

two terrorists finish their trap. A little goalie conceals the soft-tossed dirt with his goal-post rock. He gives a thumbs-up. Language doesn't speak the truth for violence. A

missile, God's fist, punches the soccer field. Broiled, blackened dirt blooms into a dying star. Bare feet and bright smiles evaporate, beneath the bridges of paper-mache confetti.

But you don't tell her that. You don't want to frighten the girl in blue. All you can say to her is, *Thank you.*

Cover Me

Bruce Barrow

I'm a dumbass. That's what Aunt Patti tells me. But she's the one who handed me the suntan lotion instead of the sunscreen two days ago so I'm the one burned to sweet Jesus and no I ain't going to Urgent Care when the fridge is full of beer.

I'll be fine tomorrow.

Just in general Aunt Patti remembers things different than I do. And then there are the things I seen that she'll never have to see. The things no one should ever have to see. So she can call me whatever she wants. I don't let that kind of thing bother me now. I'm not who I was when I went away, every one of us can agree on that. But they say I talk too much about it. That it's all I talk about. So shut up, Michael. We're tired of war and guns. I get it. They weren't there. They weren't there and they just don't fucking know.

But maybe it's worth knowing that from the roof of Patti's house I could cover the whole valley. That's something could save their lives one day, not that I'm gonna make anything of it.

Family is here from all around. California, Oregon, Kansas. Patti's got the big house and the pool so everybody piles in for the week. All the kids are in the water. Sawyer and Connor are in the water too, but I made them put on t-shirts and hats after I put a shitload of sunscreen all over them. They didn't get burned as bad as I did, at least there's that.

When Sawyer goes flying off the board with his floaties on everybody cheers. Four years old and he ain't afraid of nothin'.

I'm having a beer with my cousin Emily from L.A. who's been a vegetarian her whole life and I'm trying to get her to go fishing with me tomorrow when I see Sawyer and his little cousin Lucy painting Aunt Paula's toenails. Paula and Patti are just talking and laughing and Lucy and Sawyer are kneelin' down with a bunch of bottles of nail polish and newspaper like what they're doing is the most important thing in the world. When I come up to them I can see that each toe is a different color.

"Hey, Michael," Paula says. "How's it look?"

First of all, I'm not stupid. I can see that Paula's having fun and the kids are having fun and what we're in the middle of is a family summer day. People are in the pool and some are sitting in the shade and Frank is lighting the grill and all I have to do is say, "Good job, Sawyer. Looks good." But there's more to it than that, and I'm tired of it. There's Barbie dolls and dresses and make-up and it just never ends and all the women are fine with it. No surprise, then, when what I do say is, "That looks good and queer, son."

Aunt Paula who was smiling just a half-second before looks like she's going to kill me and all of the noise and splashing goes quiet and nineteen or so of my cousins and aunts and uncles are watching to see what I do or say next. Sawyer looks up at me like I'm not even there then goes back to brushing turquoise polish on Paula's big toe. Three seconds later though he drops the brush on the newspaper and runs for it.

He's small but he's a fast little booger. He's around the table and into the house before I can move. Not that I tried to grab him, or even think I needed to, but everybody is waiting for me to go after him and

Rachel is gonna hear all about this before she gets home from work, so, except for being surrounded and alone, I got nothing to worry about.

How long all this takes to go through my mind can't be too long, but goddammit if the next thing we see ain't Sawyer sitting on Aunt Patti's roof.

"Hey, son!" I shout at him. "What're you doin' up there?" Like I don't know this is the dumbest thing I've ever said. Like he's gonna answer, which he don't. He sees me, he's staring right at me from the peak of the roof with his knees wrapped in his arms, shooting me all the disgust somebody his size can muster.

"Good work," Paula says to me.

"Go get him, Michael," Patti says. "What the hell is wrong with you?"

Which I can feel is the sentiment of whole damn congregation. A fire they'd throw me into hotter than the sunburn under my shirt. "Shit," I say not meaning to be heard. Then, "Stay where you are, Sawyer. I'm comin' up."

"Be gentle with him," Paula says.

She knows the look I give her means shut the hell up but there's not time for this now.

Like all the houses around here the window only opens a few inches. Plenty for Sawyer, and I'm skinny, but with my sunburn and the pretzel I need to turn myself into Sawyer gets to watch me suffer for a good five minutes before I climb out next to him.

"Easy there, boy," I say, not moving too close. But he scoots closer to the edge anyway. Down below come a couple of gasps then nothing else but the quiet you hear when something might go wrong. I get that. I know that better than anybody here ever will. I'm skilled in silence. But right now, on this roof with Sawyer, I'm not so sure.

He's just a little guy, sunburned and sitting ten feet away from me. He's barefoot, wearing his baggies and a red t-shirt that says Ouachita Chargers—the high school we all went to. In ten years that'll go way too fast he'll go there too. 'Course right now he won't even look at me, squirms on the peak of the roof because he can never sit still. I see the different colors of nail polish on his fingers from his sloppy work on Aunt Paula's toes.

Basically, I don't know what the fuck to say. So we just sit here together on the roof, looking for the enemy in the valley that rolls out below us. Sawyer maybe a butt cheek from the edge. Not afraid of nothin', except maybe me.

Child Care

first published in *Volume XX*

Margaret Malone

When Maxine left she took the station wagon, some clothes, and her curling iron. Everything else I got. That first night, I smoked half a pack of stale Pall Malls that I found in her bedside table, and I hadn't smoked since the Navy. I threw up right after. So now I'm smoking again. Not so smart at my age, but who's left to care? Hal said that I had to keep moving, that was the trick. Forward motion, he said. That's when he had the idea about me watching those kids.

Hal's a security guard at the community center, and the two of us were sitting on a green bench at the park there, watching all these dogs running around while their owners stood on the grass holding leashes. Hal was in his uniform. It was the first time I'd left the house for something other than orange juice or a TV dinner in a month. The world felt like sandpaper against my skin.

Hal said the deal was for Friday nights. "Fridays, it's AA in the gymnasium," he said, "and some of the drinkers, you know, they need to bring their kids to those meetings. But, they're not allowed in."

"Yeah, that'd be disruptive," I said.

"No, not that," he said. "Because of confidentiality."

Then I said, "What happened to the guy who did it before?"

"Jimmy. He got a gig working the door at a bar on Olympic."

I told Hal I don't know. I mean, it didn't sound all that great.

"What am I supposed to do with the kids?" I said. "I don't know kids."

Hal said, "Just keep them busy at the playground here. Keep them safe until the meeting's over."

I didn't say anything. I watched a big black dog pee onto the trunk of a tree.

Hal said, "It pays about forty bucks depending on donations and the meetings are about an hour or two, depending on if they're talking after." He was slow getting up from the bench.

"You're old," I told him.

Hal said, "Let me talk to someone. If it's not you, it's gonna be some other guy so you might as well say yes."

That first Friday night I showered and put on fresh slacks. Don't ask me why I wanted to look good for those damn kids. I parked the truck in the lot and I didn't see Hal anywhere. The community center was all lit up from the inside and the main double doors were propped open, a few folks starting to head in.

I walked through the open doors, my shoes squeaking on the gym floor. A bald guy wearing a nametag that said Stu sat behind a table. I told him I was Frank and I was here to watch the kids, and he said, you're Hal's buddy, and I said, yup, Frank, that's me. He said that it's usually only three or four kids, and thanks for helping out, and I better go wait outside on the grass to round them up before heading off to the playground.

It was pretty dark out by then and sure enough there were a couple of kids hanging out on the front lawn, a bigger one, a boy with a lot of ears, and a littler one, a girl with messy pigtails. I asked if they had parents in the meeting.

The bigger one said, "Our mom." He pointed to a white lady wearing a too-big sweatshirt smoking a cigarette in front of the open doors.

I said, "So Jimmy normally watches you right?"

The littler one, the girl, said, "Where's Jimmy?"

I said, "I guess I'm Jimmy now. My name's Frank."

The boy with big ears said he was Andre and his sister was Amanda and *frank* is what his grandpa calls a hot dog.

Amanda said, "How old are you?"

"Old," I said. "Very old."

She said she was eight and Andre was nine and what did I like better cats or dogs.

"I don't know. They're both okay," I said. "You think anyone else is coming?"

Andre said, "We have to wait for Rudy. He always comes with his mom and sometimes his mom's boyfriend too."

"I like Rudy," Amanda said.

After a couple weeks, I settled into the routine pretty quick. When everyone's arrived we walk around back to the park where there's a playground. It's dark as hell by the time we're out there and as soon as we get to the play area they take off their little shoes and socks so they don't get sandy. I stand by the oak tree under one of the park's streetlamps and smoke cigarettes and make sure the kids don't fall or hurt one another too much until the meeting is over, and then I bring them back to the grass in front of the gym's double doors where I hand the kids back to their parents and collect my forty bucks. Sometimes I think about taking my shoes off too, the sand between my toes might feel good, but Maxine always said I had ugly old man feet and I don't want to scare the kids. Sometimes I push them on the swings, or wait at the bottom of the slide. Tag. Hide-and-Seek. Red-Light, Green-Light. One time Amanda didn't want to play anything at all, so we stood under the streetlamp, her small hand in mine, and we watched the boys rough-housing in the sand.

Problem was, I got to thinking about the parents in the meetings, their kids out here killing time in a dark playground, all of us waiting around for those folks to get their shit together. There's no way a kid could understand.

So tonight I bring something easy. I think maybe it could help. I don't worry about them telling. Nobody lies like the children of drunks.

We hide in the caterpillar tunnel over the sand, the one that connects the red plastic slide with the wobbly bridge. I have to duck my head to get inside and my bones creak when I bend my body to fit. The four of us sit in a row, squashed together.

Something easy, no bourbon, or schnapps.

I pull the two cans from the inside pocket of my jacket. I pop a can open, take a sip, and pass it down the line.

"I don't think we're supposed to have that," Rudy says.

"It's okay. I'm going to show you something," I say. "Take a sip, if you want."

Rudy nods his small head and smiles. Amanda doesn't say anything. She gets real quiet. Rudy is just holding the can; he hasn't sipped it yet. I pop the other can open for me.

"Andre," I say. "You started drinking yet with your friends?" I ask. "It's okay. You can tell me." He shakes his head and gives me a look like, don't be ridiculous. Rudy hands the can off to Andre and he puts his little mouth up to the can and drinks. His face scrunches up. "This is nasty," he says. He takes another little sip.

"Not too fast," I say. "Not too much."

I love these damn kids. It's easy to misunderstand. "Everyone warm enough?" I ask. Sure, I give them a cigarette. I light it, just one; we share. The smoke wafts around in the tunnel.

Amanda starts coughing. "I have asthma," she says.

"Sorry," I say. I put it out. "Okay, that was a bad idea. Sorry."

They take nibble-y sips from their beer. Andre and Rudy passing the can back and forth.

Andre says, "Isn't beer supposed to be cold?"

Rudy says, "It kind of tastes gross."

"I brought pretzels," I say. To coat their stomachs, but also to help set the scene. Rudy rips the bag open, loud. He shoves a handful in his mouth and passes it down the line. I want them to understand. I try to explain what it is—how people talk in bars; the way, when you're drinking, it's like the people you're drinking with are your real friends; and how sometimes it feels like you are safer with them than you are your own family.

What it really is I guess is people just listen different in bars, they hear things better, and pretty soon things that are true you didn't even know were true just pop right out of your mouth.

In the best times, I tell them, it's like a magic bubble happens, like you're deep in space, and there's no sound but whatever true thing you're saying, and the person you're talking to is really hearing you. They're listening to your stories like they are important, like they are their stories too.

The three of them, their little faces are looking up at me. Footsteps and a jangly dog collar on the nearby path, closer and then farther away.

They say they want to hear one of my stories. My neck starts to cramp. I don't know what to say. I take a sip of warm beer.

I tell them about fishing in the little creek behind my uncle's place when I was their age and how I would stand on the muddy bank in my bare feet just hoping I wouldn't catch anything because nothing was better than the feeling of sun on my arms and the cold creek on my feet and not needing to do anything at all but wait for nothing to happen. I keep talking and eventually I get around to Maxine and how I can't say what really happened there but that, even with everything that seemed to go wrong, there was one time when we were camping in our trailer in Yosemite and the sun wasn't all the way up yet and I could just make out the tops of the campground trees against all that granite and in that moment the smell of pine and dust was just about the best thing ever of all time.

I stop talking and take a drink again. The side of the can says the beer is straight from the Rockies. That makes me melancholy. "Maxine and I camped in the Rockies once," I say.

I start to recall things that I don't want to get into. I'm just beginning to learn to forget and I don't want to undo all that hard work. These damn kids, the three of them staring at me. It's too much.

"Pass the pretzels," I say.

"You're holding the pretzels," Andre says.

"Someone else go," I say.

"I don't want to go," Amanda says. "Can I have a pretzel?"

I clear my throat and pass the bag down to her. "It's about knowing things, friendship, like that," I say. "Andre?"

He takes a quick sip of beer from the can he's sharing with Rudy. He says one time just after Halloween but before Thanksgiving he was stuck late after school because his mom forgot to pick him up.

He bummed around the playground for a bit, he tells us, but he didn't know what to do. So he started walking to the grocery store. "I know the lady who works with the fruit and vegetables. She's my neighbor. She's let me use the phone before, the one in the back by the big walk-inside refrigerator." But once he got to the store, he says, he didn't feel like going inside. It was getting cold out, he says, "But I didn't want to go home."

Instead he sat outside on the automated mini carousel and wished he had a quarter to make it go. Then a kid came along.

"He had food stuck on his face, like dried peanut butter or something, but he had a quarter," Andre says.

The messy kid sunk his twenty-five cents in the slot and smiled at Andre. "Then he said to me, 'You wanna be friends?' and I said no. It sounds mean but, I don't know, I *didn't* want to be his friend. He seemed weird." They rode around in quiet circles for a minute until their time ran out.

"Like that?" he asks me.

I tell him, good job. Great job, kid. I try to shift position so I'm not so scrunched up in the tunnel. My cramped neck is really killing me now and my feet are starting to get cold. "Who's next?" I say.

Amanda says, "I don't want to go." Her voice sounds tired.

"You don't have to, honey," I say. "Rudy? It's getting late. You want a turn?"

Rudy says he doesn't want any more beer but can he tell a story and I say, sure thing. He tells us about a time when he burnt his hand on the stove while making hot chocolate.

His mom's boyfriend didn't think Rudy's accident required much attention so the boyfriend continued to finish his crossword puzzle at the kitchen table and Rudy says that's when he decided to hate him forever. Is that good, he says?

I don't like that story.

I think how one of the best things about camping with Maxine was the part about being somewhere that wasn't home. I ask the kids if they would rather be somewhere else.

"I know I would," I say.

Amanda says yes, she's getting cold.

So we pile into my truck, the old Chevy pick-up that Maxine and I used to haul the trailer from park to park. The engine turns over and that truck growls and rumbles underneath us. I crank the heater up and Amanda says that's better.

When they ask in a minute where we're going I will tell them the truth, that I don't know. The picture develops: we're all driving up the coast, stopping to eat burgers and soft-serve at a roadside stand, days at the beaches, nights around a campfire. North through California, Oregon, through Washington, even farther, whatever it takes, into Canada, Alaska, until they see. I'll show them how quiet it can be, how much space there is. For the first time in a long time a spark lights up inside me. This is just what I need, a chance to finally get back on the road.

Those damn kids, their three faces looking up at me.

If they want to go back, they can just say the word. It's up to them.

The truck grumbling underneath us.

Home or away, I'll say. It's your call.

The Queen is Dead

Miranda Schmidt

We made it with our dad on a Saturday when our mom was sleeping in. He looked it up online, "how to make a DIY ant farm," and walked us through all the steps together. First, we had to find two jars: one large and one small. Then we had to cap the small jar and fit it inside the big jar and glue it down so it wouldn't move around. This, our dad said, was so that the ants had a limited space to dig their tunnels, so we could see them. The little jar wasn't anything but a space-filler. Then we had to mix together regular dirt and sand, and then fill the space left in the larger jar with that. That's where the ants would live, our dad told us, in that narrow space between the little jar and the big jar's sides. After the dirt, our farm was ready. We just needed the ant part of it.

Our dad worked really hard to try to find the ants. He stomped around the yard, looking for hills, and, when he couldn't find any, we all took a trip to the park with a shovel and some spoons. We had other jars too, not the ant farm jars, the jars we had were smaller, baby-food sized. They were for collecting ants in so we could bring them home.

We found an anthill pretty quickly. It was big and had a ton of ants in it. They marched along in rows, tunneling down into the hill's entrances. We watched for a little bit before we started digging.

"Now, be careful," our dad said. "Don't hurt them. We want them alive, not squashed, right?"

So we dug really carefully, scooping up dirt with our spoons and putting it into our little baby food jars where the ants wriggled around trying to get themselves upright. They looked really cute and kind of helpless and maybe even a little scared which made sense. We *were* digging up their hill. And how could they know that we had a nice ant farm home waiting for them back at the house? They probably thought we were going to eat them or something.

Even after we filled up most of the baby food jars, Dad told us we had to keep digging into the hill so we could get the queen.

"She'll be close to the center," he told us. "Really deep down."

So we dug and dug and dug. Dad said that without the queen all the ants would die, and our ant farm would turn into a ghost farm real quick.

"The queen's the only one that can lay eggs," our dad said. "Without her, there can't be any new generations. Every ant hill needs a queen. Just like every family needs a mom."

"An ant mom!" we said, digging deeper and deeper. "Look for the ant mom!"

It took a while but we finally found her. She was *huge* and she crawled really slow. We were all a little afraid of her because we'd never seen any bug like her before, so we made Dad pick her up with his spoon and stick her in one of his jars.

He smiled at us then, "Great job guys! We've got ourselves an ant farm!"

We whooped and cheered all the way back to the house.

"Ant farm! Ant farm! We have an ant farm!"

Back at the house, we took the ants out of the baby food jars and spooned them, a few at a time, into the big ant farm jar. They looked a little dazed at first, which made sense because they probably had no idea where they were. They didn't know they were safe at home in our ant farm. They just knew that they'd been passed from spoon to jar and spoon to jar and jostled around all the way home, and they weren't in their anthill anymore. But when we put the queen in (last of all, we made our dad do it) they started to perk up. They all gathered around her like they were taking directions. And then they started digging tunnels in the dirt. And we could *see* them because of the little jar inside the big jar that made the space of dirt so narrow. This meant that the ant's tunnels bumped up against the glass and we could watch them burrow. It took a long time. They dug the tunnels grain by grain and then sometimes the tunnels caved in, and they had to dig them out again. But pretty soon, with all the ants working, they had a whole network of tunnels, a whole web of them going around and around the jar. They put the queen down near the bottom where we guessed they thought she'd be safest. And she just sat there, not moving much at all even though she was the biggest ant of all of them and probably the strongest, and if she'd helped the little ants, we thought, they'd probably have their tunnels all done in no time.

At noon, Dad made us peanut butter and jelly sandwiches with all the crusts cut off, and we started asking about Mom because she was still in their bedroom, and we hadn't seen her all day.

"Mom's not feeling too great," Dad told us, and we had to stop ourselves from telling him that Mom never felt too great lately, that he didn't know because he was at work, but we knew, even if they didn't want us to, that *something* was wrong. We saw her swallowing the little blue pills every morning with a whole cup of coffee before driving us to school without saying much of anything and hardly even looking at us, and we knew that we'd had to wait after school three times last week because she'd forgotten so the school secretary had had to call to remind her to pick us all up, and when we got home, she'd gone back to bed and shut the door without even making a snack like she used to. We didn't tell because we didn't want to get her in trouble, but we still *knew*.

But Dad started telling us about different types of ants like carpenter ants and fire ants (which were huge and deadly) and so we got distracted, and, for a while, we forgot that we knew anything at all except a whole lot about ants.

What we were supposed to do now with the ant farm was, wait for the queen to lay eggs. Dad said that once the ants got all settled into their new home, if we fed them enough, they'd start making new ants. They had to make new ants, Dad said, because their lifespans weren't that long. We'd get to see whole generations, multiple ones, within a few months. Dad seemed to think that was really cool and exciting, and we all wanted to know how baby ants looked because we didn't think we'd ever seen those before, so we started going through the kitchen trying to figure out what ants would like to eat. Dad said that fruit would be good but we thought that sounded pretty boring, so we decided to sneak them potato chips when Dad wasn't looking. We took them from the bottom of an almost empty bag so they were already pretty small and then we crumpled them into the jar. Then we waited, watching for the ants to find them, while we licked salt and grease from our fingers.

The ants found them really quickly, and they came up to the surface and picked up the potato chip pieces and took them down into the tunnels, and suddenly all the ants seemed to have little pieces of potato chips on their backs, and a bunch of them were heading down to where the queen was and laying their potato chip pieces in front of her, like they were *feeding* her. And the queen just sort of stood there with her big pile of potato chips, but we thought she looked grateful, if an ant could look anything really.

When Dad made pasta for dinner, Mom still wasn't up, so he knocked on the door really quietly and then went in with a bowl for her. We listened from the hallways and her voice sounded really small and quiet and flat and not like her voice at all, except that that was her voice a lot lately, that new small quiet flat sound, but it hadn't been, not before, at least we didn't think it had. Maybe we didn't remember right. Maybe she'd always been like this, not coming out of the bedroom, small quiet flat-voiced. Maybe that was just our mom and we'd never noticed.

When our dad came out of the bedroom we asked if we could go in to see her, and he shook his head no and said Mom needed her rest, and maybe we could see her in the morning once she'd slept. So, in the morning, we all got up early and went to the kitchen, and got down the big popcorn bowl from on top of the cupboards, and opened two big bags of potato chips, and emptied them into it. And then we all went to our parents' bedroom, and we knocked on the door really quiet and gentle like we'd seen Dad do the night before, and then we opened the door and held out the bowl of potato chips and said "We brought you breakfast in bed!" because we thought that that might make her happy because breakfast in bed was what you were supposed to do to make moms happy, and we knew that potato chips sure made us happy.

Dad sat up and rubbed his eyes like he'd just woken up, and Mom just sort of blinked at us with her skin really pale and her hair really dull looking and her face her face looking not really like her face but sort of fuzzy like smeared ink on notebook paper that had been caught in the rain, and her eyes looking at us but not really at us. It was her eyes that scared us because her eyes sort of looked like she wasn't really in them. They had that blank look that dead people eyes have on TV.

Dad got really quiet and calm, and took us out of the room.

"Mom needs some rest, okay?" he told us.

We asked him if Mom was dying, and he smiled at us and said, "No, of course not. She's just not feeling well."

But we weren't letting him off that easy this time, so we asked, "How not well? Where not well? Like a tummy ache or a sore throat?"

And Dad sighed and sat down on the couch as if we'd just made him really really tired and said, "Sometimes people don't feel well in their heads."

"Like a headache?" we asked, and Dad sighed again, which made us feel suddenly scared, so we asked if Mom had a brain tumor, which made Dad laugh a laugh that didn't sound like his.

"Sometimes grown-ups just get really sad," he told us, so we started thinking up ways to make her happy again like face-painting and funfairs and cotton candy and flowers.

But Dad said it wasn't that simple, and he told us to go and check on the ant farm, so we did. We still had the bowl of potato chips, so we started crumpling them into the jar, and the ants came up to get them and brought them down to their queen, and we crumpled more, and they came to get those, so we crumpled even more. And we started eating the potato chips ourselves, and kept crumpling and crumpling until the ant farm was full of little potato chip pieces moving down the tunnels, piling on the surface, piling down at the bottom of the jar with the queen. And we kept eating and eating and eating until our mouths felt coated with grease, and our tongues ached with salt.

When Dad called us to breakfast, we just kind of sat at the table and stared at the pancakes he'd made, feeling sick. He asked us if we were okay, and we said we just weren't feeling well so he told us we could go watch TV. We watched it for hours, way past when Saturday morning cartoons were over, and the old reruns of *The Andy Griffith Show* and *The Mary Tyler Moore Show* and *Matlock* had started. We kept watching through all of them until they started playing movies, and even then we kept watching. The house was really quiet all day. Occasionally Dad would come through the living room to check up on us, and he'd sit on the arm of the couch until the next commercial break when he'd leave to go back into his study to work or back into the bedroom to check on Mom.

In the evening, we went to check on our ant farm, and it was weird because none of the ants were really moving all that much, and some of them were completely still, like they were frozen. There were still potato chip pieces all over the farm, on top of the jar, in the tunnels, piled up down by the queen. And the queen wasn't moving at all. She was completely still with her legs really stiff looking, and a couple ants were moving around her, kind of jittery, like they were scared or worried about her and that made us scared.

We ran to get our dad and he came to check and we waited out in the living room because we knew what had happened, and we didn't want to see it anymore.

"I'm afraid the queen's dead," Dad said and we'd already known that, but his saying it made it seem really real and sad and awful.

We waited for Dad to say something about the potato chips, about how we'd probably killed her, about how it was all our fault, but he didn't. He just patted us on the heads and shoulders and said maybe we could try again next weekend.

"We'll drive out to the park with Mom," he said. "And get a whole bunch of tough lakeside ants."

The Last Bad Day of Fourteen Years

Daniel Edward Moore

Night fell   on the last bad day   of fourteen years
a charred thumb   blistered   by a tiara of lighters
flickering out   like an Afghan sky
rinsed clean   by the tears   of Midwest boys
mourning the absence   of mothers and corn
mothers who would   have prayed   for my eyes
like Nuns in   the Covent   of blind yesterdays

You were   my tourniquet   my nylon savior
my artist in residence   painting air on my lungs
You are   why truth   is only a scar
a place where   fingertips touch   to make temples
where relief arrives   like a foreign plane
skidding off the runway   one hour before dawn
before the last   bowl of me   turns to dust
in the moonlight   and tomorrow chooses   to offer its life
on behalf   of the   open hearts   waiting

My Friend's Divorce
first published in *Volume I*

Naomi Shihab Nye

I want her
to dig up
every plant
in her garden,
the pansies, the penta
roses, ranunculus,
thyme and the lilies,
the thing
nobody knows the name of,
unwind the morning glories
from the wire windows
of the fence,
take the blooming
and the almost-blooming
and the dormant,
and then
and then

plant them in her new yard
on the other side
of town
and see how
they breathe!

Parked on Ginkgo Street

Charlene Logan Burnett

Jeffrey priced his house so it wouldn't sell. When the offer came in, above the asking price, he had no choice. His lawyer, his ex-wife and her lawyers, his parents, even his own children, ganged up on him.

He parked across the street, a few lots down from the house and ate lunch. He didn't want the new family to recognize him. They'd met, crossing paths at the title company. He'd smiled at the young son, Ryan, a mere toddler. Just about the age Jeffrey's oldest was when they'd bought the house.

He had twenty minutes before heading back to work. If he ate healthier, he'd feel better, but he couldn't make himself care. He reached inside the Burger King bag. His ex-wife's voice piped up in his head. *Have you taken a good look at yourself lately?* He smashed the bag against the steering wheel. His therapist's voice chimed in. *Where is this rage coming from?*

Why shouldn't he be mad? How could he be so stupid? Nineteen years wasted. Not once had it occurred to him she'd cheat.

He was lost in that thought, recreating scenarios where he confronted Michelle and smashed her friend's face into the dirt, and it took him a moment to notice that Crosby, the neighbor's Mastiff mix, was out on the sidewalk, three orange tennis balls stuffed in his distended mouth.

Archie, Crosby's elderly owner, bent down and peered into the car. "We thought that was you."

The Mastiff jumped up, stuffed his blocky head through the open window, and dropped the tennis balls onto Jeffrey's lap.

"He wants to play," Archie said.

Jeffrey tossed the slobbery balls out. "I don't have time for nonsense."

Straightening up, Archie stepped away from the car, his bushy eyebrows raised.

Jeffrey turned the ignition and drove off.

Jeffrey bought peanuts from the vending machine. He was a draftsman at Kohl and Partners, one of the largest architectural firms in Sacramento. He'd wanted to be an artist—an illustrator, and later, an architect who specialized in remodeling historical homes. Then Michelle got pregnant while he was in graduate school. At the time, he'd been happy to give up his career and dreams. He was all for growing a family.

"Why do you think your children don't speak to you?" Jeffrey's therapist had asked.

Jeffrey knew the answer. Michelle had brainwashed them. None of them would listen to Jeffrey's side anymore.

Last winter, after driving over sixteen hours, Jeffrey had arrived at his oldest son's dorm. Growing up, J.T. had always come to his dad for advice—girls, school, career choice—but there he stood in the doorway, his arms crossed. "You're way over the top on this divorce, Dad. You've got to get hold of yourself. You're a mess."

Boulder was colder than Sacramento, and Jeffrey had bundled up in a couple of sweatshirts he kept for rags in the trunk. Jeffrey needed a pair of warm dry boots. A sweater. A cup of cocoa, spiked with whisky. And a few compassionate words—*Dad, I don't know how mom could have done that to you. She was so wrong. It was evil.* Instead, J.T. handed him a blanket and pillow. "You can crash on the floor, but you got to be out by morning. University housing rules."

Now, as Jeffrey sat in front of his office computer, he yelled out, "Who do you think's paying for your education and that room?"

Kyle, the draftsman who worked at the table closest to Jeffrey, lifted his hand and shook his wrist out, but didn't comment. He was like all the others. First, feigning sympathy, then, pretending to listen. Finally, rolling his eyes and walking away. Even his retired parents, who had absolutely nothing to do all day, would say when he called, "Sorry, son, you caught us at a bad time."

Which was fine. Jeffrey had learned a whole lot about human nature lately. People liked winners. Michelle was the winner. She packed up and moved herself and their youngest son into the boy-friend's house, which had a swimming pool and a Jacuzzi. When Jeffrey fought for custody, all three of his kids stood by their mother in court.

Jeffrey clicked a menu on his computer screen and dragged and dropped a row of lockers into the CADD blueprint of an elementary school. He had squandered his artistic talents. He couldn't remember the last time he'd pulled out his sketchpad and put charcoal to paper. When the kids were young, his own creative direction didn't seem to matter. Instead, he found happiness with his family, his children. He drew wall-size murals in each of their rooms. J.T. wanted bi-winged airplanes. Margie was into cats and dogs. Marshall, the youngest, and the one who'd stuck by Jeffrey the longest after the divorce, told his dad, "Surprise me!"

It took Jeffrey weeks to piece together the routine of the new family. While out of the office, dropping off blueprints or meeting an architect at a site, he'd swing by the house. The man left each weekday morning, exiting the garage in a tan Audi, between 7:15 and 7:30. Shortly after, the woman left through the side door. It was October, still warm, and she always wore pastel-colored dresses in peach, bluebell, lime sherbet. At the bottom of the steps, she'd hold out the boy's turtle-shaped backpack and slide its padded straps over his small shoulders. She walked him to Nanette's preschool. Thirty minutes later, she'd leave the house in her silver Prius.

He wasn't sure why he was noting their activities. His therapist would surely have an opinion, but Jeffrey wasn't going to tell him about it. This was his home. He'd bought it, paid the mortgage, built the second-floor addition, worn a HEPA air-filter mask while single-handedly removing the asbestos-laced popcorn ceiling. He had a right to what he had worked for his whole life. Or at least to savor it just a little while longer.

Drowsy after lunch, he pushed his seat in the car back. The street was quiet except for voices resounding out from the preschool play yard. All three of his children had attended Nanette's. He'd served on its parent participation committee. He'd painted many of the classrooms. The teachers had even presented him with a framed thank you plaque and a twenty-five dollar Cattlemen's gift card.

A few months later, he and Michelle had hired a babysitter and went out on a rare date night. Michelle hadn't worked while the children were young, and while he made decent money, there was no extra for steakhouse dinners. He thought they'd both mutually agreed that they'd get the three children through college, and then it would be their turn to find that old spark between them.

Jeffrey opened his eyes. The voices from Nanette's play yard sounded less like the laughter of children and more like taunts and jeers. He rolled up his car window. He rummaged around in the paper sack for a French fry.

He'd noticed a change in Michelle around the time Marshall started looking into colleges. By then, she was working full time at the med center. She dyed her hair and eyebrows. She switched from pantsuits to short skirts and blouses. She worked late. He followed her one evening. She exited the tower building, drove her car to the EconoLodge on 16th Street, and went up to a second-floor room. He hadn't eaten lunch that day, but he leaned out his car door and barfed. That night, when he confronted her, she screamed, "I'm forty-eight years old. It's finally my turn."

Jeffrey checked his dashboard clock. He was late. He sped across town. He grabbed the schematics for the elementary school and rushed into the meeting, quickly arranging the blueprints on the oblong conference table. "Sorry, guys. Got caught in traffic."

Charles Kohl, the lead architect, dismissed the group.

"Did I miss the whole thing?" Jeffrey asked.

"Take a seat," Charles said.

"What's up?" Jeffrey tapped his fingers on the oak armrest.

"You tell me." Charles leaned back.

Jeffrey reached to loosen his collar, but stopped. It was a nervous habit that his therapist had pointed out. He let his hand drift down by his side.

"You've had a rough year," Charles said. "We understand that. We've given you a lot of leeway. You were, after all, once our best draftsman."

The walls in the room edged in closer. Jeffrey looked out the plate-glass window, coated in black film to keep out glare. The building opposite Kohl and Partners had a clock tower. He focused on the minute-hand. He took a deep breath. He looked back at Charles. "I don't feel well."

"And it's not just the quality of your work. You're hardly in the office anymore."

Jeffrey stiffened. "I don't know what you're talking about."

"You disappear for hours. No one knows where you are."

Jeffrey couldn't lose this job. "I'm having stomach problems. It hits, I have to get to a bathroom. I haven't wanted to talk about it."

"Have you seen a doctor?"

"Yes," Jeffrey lied. "It's stress related."

"Maybe you should take a few weeks off."

When Michelle moved out, her exact words: "I need a break. A few weeks. Time to think." She never returned.

Jeffrey blinked and turned in his seat so Charles couldn't see his face. The hand on the tower clock ticked forward, forward, forward. "I don't think that's necessary," Jeffrey said, clearing his throat. "And I'm neck-deep in that elementary school project."

"Kyle can pick up your load. You go home. Get some rest. We'll talk in a few weeks."

That night the phone rang, startling Jeffrey out of a deep sleep.

It was Michelle. "What is wrong with you? I got a call from Jean Kohl. She said you're out on disciplinary leave."

"That's not true." Jeffrey sprang out of bed. "I've been sick. GI problems."

"You've never had health problems."

"I've never been divorced."

"Come on. It's been over a year. You need to move on."

"Like you?"

After a pause, she spoke in a softer voice, "Jeffrey, everyone's worried about you. Especially the kids. They miss their old dad. The dad they once knew."

"They've always been welcome to come stay with me."

"You live in a dark, dingy apartment."

"It has three bedrooms."

"They're used to a nice house with a yard and lawn and trees."

"We had that. You and me. Then you ruined it." He chewed on a fingernail, an old habit.

"It's always someone else's fault."

He held his stomach as he paced. "Nineteen years. I gave up everything for you. I was going to be an artist."

"Oh, come on, Jeffrey. Grow up. You were never going to be an artist or an architect. You were looking for any excuse not to have to prove yourself."

Later, he tried to eat soup and dry crackers.

Hunched over the sink, he wondered if maybe he did indeed have a serious illness, like stomach cancer.

The next morning, at 7:30, he had nowhere to go. He ate oatmeal. It hadn't rained since April, and outside the window blackbirds bathed under a sprinkler. He doodled on the back of an envelope.

Since moving into the apartment, Jeffrey could not find his bearings. The building was built in 1903. Once an elegant home, it was now divided into a mishmash of small units. In graduate school, Jeffrey had imagined that one day, when he was a successful architect, he'd purchase a historic home and restore it to its former glory. When he signed the twelve-month lease, he had some cockeyed belief that he was in fact reclaiming a part of himself.

He had not inspected the building closely. The walls were cracked. Black mold lurked in the bathroom. The walls and trim needed paint.

The building super was outside. Jeffrey went down and pointed to the water from the sprinklers pooling near the foundation. "There's no lawn here. You're watering dirt. Now you have water seepage, which leads to hydrostatic pressure."

"Not my house. Not my problem," the super said.

Moss grew along the stone foundation, but in the back by the parking lot, Jeffrey found the clay soil bone dry. No wonder he felt off balance. The very building he lived in was tipping.

At noon, he went out to Burger King. He parked in his usual spot under the ginkgo tree and ate his crispy chicken sandwich and fries. He'd left detailed instructions for the new family about the sprinkler system, yet brown patches blighted the lawn.

He stepped out of his car.

"Hey, Jeffrey!"

Archie and Crosby had snuck up on him.

"Twice in the same week. What keeps bringing you back to the old neighborhood?"

Nosy old man. Jeffrey jiggled his keys. "Just dropping some keys off. Forgot to hand them over when we closed."

Crosby dropped his tennis balls and wagged his tail, then went back and forth, back and forth, eyeing Jeffrey and the three balls.

Jeffrey had once enjoyed playing a few rounds with his sons. When they got older and their interests changed, he was more than happy to toss one out for old Crosby.

Jeffrey patted the dog's huge black head. "Sorry. They got me on a tight leash at work. Got to go back."

Jeffrey sensed Archie and Crosby watching as he jogged across the street. At the front door, he instinctively reached for the knob, but then stepped back and rang the doorbell even though he knew no one was home. Pam worked mornings and didn't pick up Ryan until after two o'clock. Paul was an attorney. He often didn't make it home until after nine.

Through the sidelight windows, he saw they'd replaced the foyer flooring. He glanced over his shoulder. Archie and his dog were dawdling. Jeffrey pretended to slide a key through the brass mail slot. He held up his key ring to signal Archie—mission accomplished.

Archie tapped off a military salute and moved on.

Jeffrey walked slowly toward his car. When Archie and Crosby were far enough away, he doubled back.

Years ago, he'd buried a key by the back door into the garage. He unearthed the rusted tin box. He'd always been a careful man, planning ahead, scrutinizing everything from all angles. "Life is unpredictable," his therapist had told him. "You can't see the future."

Inside the garage, he closed his eyes. He breathed in the familiar scents, the cement walls, the faint whiff of gas and oil. He'd always saved cans of open paint. Matching color when touching up a bathroom or one of the murals was always so difficult. The cans were gone. He winced, imagining the man in his Audi lining the trunk with garbage bags and transporting all the cans Jeffrey had saved over nineteen years to a hazardous waste site.

The inside garage door wasn't locked. He turned the knob, stepped up—and stopped. His knotty pine kitchen cabinets were painted in white shellac.

He could hear his therapist asking, *What did you think? That they'd keep everything exactly the same?*

How could anyone paint over the warm patina of old wood?

And the paint job was sloppy. The masking tape, poorly placed. They hadn't even bothered to sand and caulk where the wrought iron hinges and pulls had worn against wood.

The oven clock displayed 12:45. He had time before Pam returned.

On the stainless steel refrigerator, magnets secured photos of Ryan and notices sent home from preschool. Friday at 6:30 was the annual school picnic. Jeffrey had always enjoyed those nights. He'd designed all the flyers for the school. Everyone remarked on how well he could draw. It was what he'd heard since he was child. Teachers marveled at his straight lines. Classmates begged him to draw cartoon characters on their canvas notebooks.

He stopped in the hall where a gallery of his children's school year portraits once hung. The flowered paper, which he'd carefully chosen because the branches matched the wooden trim, had been stripped, but not yet painted. He touched his palm to where his wedding portrait once hung. He and Michelle were in their twenties. She wore a yellow mini shift that day. She had very long legs. Her hair was golden. Her hand rested on his arm. Her body leaned in to him.

"People change," his therapist had told him.

They sure as hell do.

Jeffrey had climbed the stairway so many times, he remembered the rise and squeak of each step.

The door to Marshall's bedroom was closed, but Jeffrey knew the moment his hand touched the door handle, and a bolt like lightening sparked up his arm, that his son's 'Surprise Me' mural was gone. He stepped into the room. The rain forest with its towering trees, thick, flowering vines, and moonlit watering hole, gone. The spotted leopard, the green parrot, the tiny trees frogs he'd painted with such care, all gone.

His strength drained from his body, and he sat on the edge of the small bed, his legs sprawled out in a V.

He'd worked late so many nights on the wall so it would be finished for his son's sixth birthday. Marshall had been proud of his dad then. He'd told all his friends that his father was a great artist. The neighborhood kids begged Jeffrey to paint them a mural too, but of course, he couldn't paint everyone's walls.

The last time Jeffrey's phone calls to Marshall were answered was when he told his son that his mother was a bitch and a whore. "Dad, stop it! You're driving everyone away." Jeffrey knew he'd gone too far, but he couldn't seem to stop himself. He'd left messages, apologizing to his son, but Marshall had not yet forgiven him.

Jeffrey lay on Ryan's bed, resting his ankles across the footboard. He tapped his fingers on his stomach. When his kids were young, he was the one who read them bedtime stories. It was the best part of his day, spending time with his children, answering their many questions, holding them close. Jeffrey covered his face with the pillow and sobbed like he had those first few weeks after Michelle told him she was never coming home. "You need to move on, Jeffrey. I have."

He must have fallen asleep because when he opened his eyes and turned, a small face peered down at him. Ryan.

"Don't be scared," Jeffrey said, sitting up. "It's okay."

"Who are you?"

"I used to live here."

"In my room?"

"This was once my son Marshall's room." He looked at the blank powder-blue wall. "I painted the jungle that was there."

"My mom got rid of it."

"I can see that."

"It was scary."

"Scary?"

"There were snakes and a water buffalo. And monkeys with big teeth."

Scary? Jeffrey tried to recollect the wall from that perspective.

"RYAN!" Pam's feet pounded up the stairs. "What the hell?" She pulled Ryan to her.

Ryan tugged on his mother's sleeve. "Mom, he used to live here."

Her eyes shifted as she recognized Jeffrey. "You better get the hell out of here before I call the police."

Jeffrey couldn't remember ever feeling so low. "I'm so sorry."

She was dialing.

"I'm leaving."

"Help," she screamed into the phone. "This creep is in *my* house. In my child's bedroom."

"I'm going. I meant no harm. I just wanted to see it one last time." He was on the stairs. He was in the foyer. He was out the door. He was running to his car.

He looked back only once. Pam was out on the lawn, still on the phone, carrying Ryan, pacing. Archie and Crosby rushed through their gate. They stopped short when they saw Jeffrey.

His hands shook as he clutched the steering wheel. His mind raced with possibilities—he'd be arrested, his mug shot would be on the six o'clock news, his children, their teachers, their friends, would all see him as the creepy man who broke into people's homes and slept in their children's beds. He had to remind himself to stop at red lights. His vision was off. It was daylight, yet it seemed he was driving at night without headlights. More than once, he came dangerously close to sideswiping a parked car.

Across town, he finally slowed. He pulled over and parked. "What have I done?" he asked God, the universe, whoever or whatever was in charge of these things. His therapist's words came back to him. It was one of their first meetings. Jeffrey had sat on the couch, sobbing, clutching the Kleenex box. "You're grieving," his therapist said. "You need to journey through it. There are no shortcuts. Only time."

Time. The trees along the street had already turned bronze and yellow. The dappled sun spilled across his windshield. It was the kind of light that artists loved to capture, but had always eluded him. He closed his eyes and for the first time in a very long time, he felt warmth on his face.

Westside Fence, Kern Water Bank Sensitive Habitat Area

Don Thompson

Far off, the champagne pop
of a shotgun
celebrates another dove season;
otherwise, immaculate silence
that makes me want to hold my breath.

I'd have to call this peace,
despite the hunt
and almost at my feet,
one shamelessly red .410 shell
with a few more scattered nearby,
faded to gray—dingy
and nothing at all like
the iridescent mauve-silver buff
of the doves that got away.

Dirty Old Man in His Office

Gustavo Pérez Firmat

He has just signed his last dissertation.
Hidden away in his fourth-floor birdnest,
blinds drawn to block the city,
door locked to bar his colleagues,
walls papered with photos and clippings
to recall his fifteen minutes, maybe less,
of fame dispersed across forty years,
D.O.M. drops into his chair like a leaf.

Not that his ministry as good shepherd
of doctoral flock will make him deserve
Academy's lifetime achievement award:
two theses for each decade, a fraction
of the sums flaunted by mutton-mad peers.
Soon after he jawed and jargoned his way
to a job, he decided that departments
like his did not need people like him
before he turned into what he has been
these many years. So he kept his distance
from lithe lambs (intellectually that is)
and they from him (intellectually that is).
Mentor misses tormentor by three letters.

He never found a reason to treat students
the way he treats himself. Still he's afraid
of endings crowding every room in his life.

He slides open the top drawer of the cabinet
by the desk, reaches behind the futile files,
grabs a bottle of his power drink, Glenlivet.
Before he hurries down the stairs hoping
to see no one, he gulps a mouthful and sighs.

Job#18 Divinity

Jude Brewer

During the winter months, Donut Friday progresses to Sugar Friday where anything goes. The ladies in Pharmacy bring homemade frosted cookies and fudge brownies and the usual box of a dozen maple bars and jelly-filled heart attacks. I'm still young so I take an extra for every person claiming they're on a diet. Then a mass email alerts the warehouse there's an employee appreciation luncheon complete with ham and turkey and mashed potatoes and gravy and, as the email states, "of course, plenty of desserts." So on the way to the luncheon, I poke my head into a room with a couple half-eaten cakes, the dry chocolate kind with the cheap-tasting whipped frosting.

A single employee sits in the corner quietly eating slices of cake. I cannot remember his name despite exchanging the "hey" and "how's your day?" and "pretty good, thanks, yours?" and "pretty good, thanks" for the last year.

"Oh! Jonny, did you want some cake?"

"I'm good, thanks. Why's this all in a separate room? The luncheon's next door."

"Oh, it's my last day so they bought me this cake to share."

"Plenty to go around...but I see two cakes."

"Oh, the other one's for someone's birthday but they called in sick. Since they both just say Happy Birthday, people kinda picked at either one."

"So where're you working next?"

"Oh, the hospital down the street. It pays a lot better."

"Send me an email when you get there." I'm thinking, *then I'll know what to call you from now on besides Oh.* I walk to the luncheon, fill two plates worth of food, one mostly meat and the other mostly potato, both drowned in gravy. I spend the afternoon breaking down pallets stacked with wheelchairs and walkers until the sugar sweats through my pores and that little spot in my lower back seizes. There's a proper way to lift, but it requires lifting consciously, and, most of the time, I'm moving too fast to weigh the safety of my movements. Maybe that's dangerous and will catch up to me, but until it does I'm accident-free and everything is fine.

5:30 p.m., the UPS guy still isn't here. James calls their dispatch and urges them to hurry over since he's paying me overtime to stick around. When the driver does arrive, James asks, "You know FedEx and UPS are merging, don't you?"

The driver is shocked. "Where'd you hear that?"

James looks to me then back at him. "It was all over the news. They're merging, and word is they're rebranding themselves as Fed-Up." He snickers and makes this pose where he bunches his arms together like he's standing in the fetal position or getting ready to pitch. The driver is shaking his head, and it only gets a bigger laugh out of James.

The warehouse doors get closed, the lights shut off, and I clock out. It's a quarter past six when James stops me.

He says, "I hope you know you're loved."

James is referring to Jesus Christ and his Father, Papa Christ. He's also referring to himself and whoever else might be in my life that may love me without me knowing. He's not a church pastor but the role would more appropriately suit him over Warehouse Supervisor or Manager.

He says, "I prayed for you the other night. I know you're going through something lately and it's none of my business what that is. But I want you to know you're a great man, and you've done a lot for this place. For us. And we love you for it."

It doesn't make a difference whether I tell him I don't believe in any gods or emotional delusions akin to any meanings of love. He can talk to himself in the evenings and pretend it's a direct line to his deity's voicemail all he wants.

"Thanks, James. Have a good weekend."

I want to shrink away from his hug, but I don't want his feelings hurt. His burly arms wrap around me in such a way that I know his words are genuine. And as much as I just want to leave this warehouse behind and drink away the weekend, if I close my eyes I can imagine we're not in Oregon but instead in Arizona. It's summer, not winter. And Dad isn't some homeless addict sleeping at the mall preaching but instead he's a middle manager of a warehouse for durable medical equipment, and anytime I need some reassurance he's there to say, "You're doing everything you can and everything you're supposed to."

6:30 p.m., down the street at the Chinese dive bar. Eating now means I won't get sloshed early enough, and a new waitress is working the bar and keeps smiling, and I've already convinced myself she's interested in coming over later. She checks my ID, says, "Nice smile." Her friendliness has nothing to do with how many drinks can be bought with however much is on my credit card because the debit's overdrawn but that won't stop me from having a fun time. Future Me's stuck paying all the way to the Great Dirt Nap anyhow, so heap on another grand! He can take it. He can probably make it downtown before this last shot kicks in. Phone buzzes. *Over on Alberta if you still want to meet up for drinks.* The waitress asks, "One more shot before closing out?" "Of course." The charge is approved, and he's in his car, now he's texting. A girl is in the passenger seat. It's dark enough, no one sees or maybe they do. Someone's watching. The window's rolled down part way. Whatever. He's already forgotten her name and a condom and his plans to write for that upcoming anthology all of his friends are likely to be published in. He says, "I gotta go." She's out of the car and he's at an ATM then he's in a shower washing his hair with lavender scented shampoo, and a pair of hands with painted nails helps. He's on a bed of purple sheets kissing the stripper from just a few, how many was that, when? She says, "Thanks sometimes for later again call you don't hear if." It's dark out or getting light. His smartphone says it's Saturday, not Friday. He's at a bar scribbling words on whiskey, no allegiance to any drink but whatever is familiar or isn't anything he's tried before. He balances each sip with half a page then two sips a page then a drink for a sentence. He wanders over to his car until he's not. He's somewhere on the other side of town trying to buy a drink, but he can't find his damn credit card. He's back on the last bar closing his tab and getting his card, and he's pissed off enough he doesn't care he's only got four-hundred left. He sits in his car scrolling through escort ads on his smartphone. The ATM lets him pull out two-fifty, and the two girls are young enough they don't try and negotiate so they take turns on him until they're out of breath and he's ready to be alone and write now. But the apartment is silent. The roommates are gone for the weekend for whatever holiday it is where people eat a shit ton of food with their dads and moms and sisters and brothers and aunts and uncles and cousins and grandmas and grandpas. Another hour's left until the bar down the street closes so he empties the can of quarters he spends on the bus and spends it all on another drink he's familiar with or never tried before. His Saturday is Sunday, and he's downtown with a writer friend at the entrance to a hotel bar. The bouncer asks to see his ID. It's missing. The bouncer says, "Just go in. You're good." The writer friend twice his age is buying every drink until they're sitting closer then they're parked outside her place, no words left to share, but really he's out of words these days. He sleeps and dreams of breaking down pallets of wheelchairs and walkers in his apartment living room, calling in sick because he can't get through to the front door to get to work to break down more pallets. He wakes up late, skips the shower, and makes it to the warehouse just in time to grab the last maple bar. It's Donut Monday, after all.

A Barstool at St. Nicks

Fred Dale

The church pew says we are all in this together,
but the barstool's singularity gets it right.
I listen to the scuffed skeleton of nervous kicks—
prefer sitting on the head of a pin, facing the pit,
the rambled confusion of one-sided conversations,
the effervescent smoke's grey notes, thinking done
in the darkening wells of the lungs. It's a day's
drinking and this is mercy work. I've seen priests
set the paten over the open cup of the blood
to keep it safe from God knows what, and as I
teeter slightly from your arms to the beaten path
of elimination, I do the same with a napkin on my
beer—a chip to keep me in the game. I'll be back.
Wait for me in the momentum, won't you?
Come closing time, a man in an unwinding tux
will sing for us *Happy Trails*, a bedtime story
for St. Nick's bar, but only then, as he croons out
the truth of night's end, does the barstool change
into a horse that I realize I've been riding steadily
all along—at some heavenly pace, the sun never
quite able to get away from the jerking horizon.
And there's a spot on the sun that turns out to be

a desiccating roach no one has bothered to remove
from the panel lights above the bar, a six-legged
hourglass we measure our successes against.
Saddles are personal, and really, if you want
to know, the barstool's an easel. Can't you see it,
the likeness, the crass caricature? We are painted
corners where occasionally men will stand to
drink, elbows back in support and staring self-
assuredly at the walk-in life. A word of caution
to you, interlopers: don't meddle in our careers.
It's a long haul. Watch this rotting carousel for
a while before you jump on. There's a barstool
just for you, the gallant rush of centrifugal force.
Put your ear between the sounds of our failings
and listen for your place. You'll know the one.
Instead of a boutique brew, let your arms end
in a prayer of folded hands and an Irish whiskey.
There's always something to get to here.

If It's Going to Happen Anyway, I Want to Feel It

John Sibley Williams

Dust, mostly. And pale wood offcuts.
Shredded paper no longer coarse enough
for smoothing edges. Remnants of enduring things
litter the base of our temporary object. Sometimes

I can't tell if this is a house made for birds
or spice jars. If this house was built from the ruin
of others. But I must own it. Like how father's sweater
owns the smell of wood smoke and old sunlight.

How our garage is open to a cul-de-sac owned by
children who even after the training wheels come off
will endlessly circle the same safe bit of pavement.
How I was one of those children, once.

Like how Grandpa owns the coal in his lungs
and still rubs the empty space where his arm should be.
*It's a dangerous game, making something useful
from nothing,* he says through a mouthful of midnight

and cancer. Of nail and hammer and country. Sometimes
I want to run the tree of my body over the table between us
to make it useful. To make a house for my coming ruin.
The saw spins so slowly, I fear my hands may never sever.

The Parable of the Gun

first published in *Volume XI*

Stephen Graham Jones

We locked him in the old fitting rooms because he said he was Jesus. And because it was the end of our shift.

"Save *them*," Marco said to him through the louvered doors, and swept his hands to all the naked mannequins the fitting rooms were already storing, their arms in every posture of worship.

Jesus pulled his face over the top of the door, rested his bearded chin on the backs of his fingers, and watched us. He wasn't even mad about the way we'd tackled him off the cosmetics display pad. How the customers had laughed and clapped and then turned away, embarrassed. What Marco had threatened to do to all that long hair. What I had done with the leather sandal that had been left on the display pad, as if Jesus had just been transubstantiated up to the second floor. Lingerie, probably.

It was as close as there was to heaven at Dunlap's.

In the security booth we spent the rest of our shift with sticky notes, putting one on each monitor, telling Jarret and Kale, the night shift, that Jesus was their problem now. Through the walkie-talkie Marco had left keyed open by the fitting rooms, we could hear Jesus humming. It wasn't even a hymn, just a song from the radio.

"We should throw him to the lions," Marco said, smiling to himself, wheels turning in his head that hadn't turned in a long time.

"You mean Delaney and Gale?" I said, after checking behind me.

Delaney and Gale were the area coordinators, the bosses when the manager wasn't on the floor. They took it very seriously. Marco hissed through his teeth, dotted an *i* on some complicated insult he'd been writing to Jarret and Kale, then fixed it on the last empty screen. He nodded to himself, satisfied with his work, and leaned back in the ergonomic chair we'd had to make special requests for.

Jesus still humming, the dial tone of his voice starting to break into words in places. The lyrics would be next.

"He didn't have headphones, did he?" Marco said.

"Gale's going to hear him," I said back, nowhere to put my eyes now that all the monitors were covered.

Marco focused his attention on the walkie-talkie again.

"Watch this," he said, and palmed it, thumbed the line open. Said in his deepest, most resounding voice, "Son, this is God, your father. Don't make me come down there again."

The humming trailed off, got swallowed.

I shook my head, looked out the small, wire-mesh glass window set in the steel door of our security booth.

"We're going to hell now," I said to Marco. "You know that, right?"

Marco laughed, stood. Said, "This place isn't hell, I don't want to see it, man," then started unpacking his belt into his locker, shouldering into his jacket. I fell in, standing my pepper spray on the top shelf of my locker, hanging my stick from the hook. Charging the batteries on my hand-held. The one we'd left by the fitting rooms with Jesus was Jarret and Kale's problem, now. Let them charge it.

Walking out, my foot stopping the door for Marco to ease through, I almost saw something on the monitors, I thought. All the sticky notes, though. I couldn't be sure.

"What?" Marco said.

"Goodnight," Jesus said, clearly, though the walkie-talkie. As if his beard were right up to it, rustling into the receiver holes.

"Shit," Marco said, drawing his lips up from his teeth. "I see a donkey in the parking lot, my dumb ass is calling in tomorrow."

I pulled the door locked behind us.

Jesus was Jarret and Kale's problem now.

Part of the end of rounds—what the OP called it when security was clocking out—was making a final circuit of the store, to be sure what you were handing off to the next shift was as safe and secure as you could make it. It was a useless procedure, of course: on the way to the time-clock, not only were we in our civvies, but our spray and sticks and walkie-talkies were back in the box. It kind of made any kind of walk-through useless. Except for Jeanine, of course, the built-for-sin holy roller in Misses, who for some reason thought we were real cops, or cops in training, or something. It didn't matter. If we got there at 8:45, she'd already be zoning her area, squaring all the shirts onto their aisle displays, fluffing collars, refolding pants. To one degree or another, of course—because of Delaney and Gale—everybody at least went through the motions of zoning. Not everybody wore blouses as loose and low-cut as Jeanine, though. All you had to do while she folded was stand there, and, bam, suddenly the last eight hours had been worth it.

"Guess you heard we caught your boy today," Marco said to her, his right arm cocked up on a rounder, "Jesus I mean."

Jeanine looked up to him, then me.

I nodded, said, "The real one."

She shook her head, smiled, and said "we must be real Philistines then, right?"

Over her shoulder, Marco bored his eyes into me, waiting for a signal, to know if being a Philistine was good or bad.

"That a commandment?" I said to Jeanine.

In reply she hit me lightly on the shoulder and I acted like it was a roundhouse, folded over the register in fake pain, then, walking through Housewares minutes later, realized that I should have played along, gone farther, should have spun her around by the wrist, her arm behind her, as if I were apprehending her. It would have pulled her right up against me.

That's why I was working security at a department store, though: because my whole life had already been a series of not thinking of things in time, when they could have done some good.

At the end of the Housewares, the final stretch to the timeclock, me and Marco both saw the trenchcoat guy, already turning away from us, the tails of his black coat swirling around like the cape of a superhero.

Marco pretended just to be looking straight ahead.

"You care?" he said.

"Amateur," I said back, about the trenchcoat guy, and like that we let him slide, didn't want to do the paperwork he was obviously going to require. All he was stealing was plates or saucers or something anyway. For his grandmother, what? It didn't matter. Fine china wasn't why the store had gone full-time with security last year. There wasn't really a market for hot saucers, nice forks. What there was a market for, however, always, was electronics. It's why we kept them in a chain-link cage in back now, locked with a set of keycodes that the computer kept track of somehow. It didn't stop the handheld stuff from walking out of the store, but it did make it walk slower, anyway. Sometimes in our pockets even, which management, having gone to special workshops about, learned to expect. The way they dealt with it was to try to buy our loyalty, show we were part of the family—that it was our stuff too. What they tried to buy our loyalty with was a twenty-percent discount on all electronics that weren't on clearance. To get that twenty percent though, we had to use a charge card. Which is to say the store owned us, more or less. Had even cut off the ten percent discount all the floor employees got, for work clothes. Cut it off and still made us stick to their stupid-ass dress code: black slacks, shirts with at least three buttons, not counting the sleeves.

What we could have done with the trenchcoat guy, I guess, was lock him up with Jesus.

What we did instead was home in on that timeclock, lean against the wall around it with unlit cigarettes in our mouths, the third shift cleaning crew waiting there as well, to clock in.

"Say a prayer," Marco told me, lifting his chin to the timeclock that was taking hours, not minutes.

I looked at it hard, nodded, and said, "I wish I may, I wish I might—" and then didn't get to finish.

From the floor, a woman was screaming.

Marco closed his eyes, thinned his lips, and shook his head no, please, but it didn't matter: we were still clocked in.

Before following him back through Hardware, I balanced my cigarette on top of the timeclock, shook my head no to the custodial staff. That that was *my* cigarette.

When I turned to take the impact of the aluminum doors Marco had left swinging though, my cigarette was already gone, the custodial staff all just standing there with their hands in their pockets, no eye contact.

Of course I didn't believe our guy in the old fitting rooms was really Jesus.

In my eight months at Dunlap's, the eight months since the other security crew had gone up on grand larceny charges, there'd been a total of two screaming women. Just absolutely hysterical. I mean, unstoppable. If we could have restrained them, we would have, maybe. Instead, because the women had been screaming due to some bad or good news they'd just got on their phones—a death the first time, an engagement the second—we'd let the women on the floor talk them down. Sit with them until they were just sobbing, then lead them away. Knowing the girls on the floor, sell them something along the way.

This third screaming woman was a whole different scene.

It was Gale.

She was on her knees at the intersection of the two main aisles, where the tile was still rough from the watch stand that had been pulled up from there my first week on.

She was screaming because the man in the trench coat was standing behind her, a large chrome pistol held to the back of her head.

I slowed down my run.

"Do it!" the trenchcoat man called out across Misses, and I followed his voice to Delaney.

Her key was in the console that dropped the cages on all the exits.

She turned it, the ceiling shook, and the trenchcoat man smiled, and together we watched all the rounders move like savannah grass, when you know the small, tasty animals are moving away just beneath it.

In turn, one by one, the trenchcoat man waited for the shoppers to make their last scuttle from the make-up counter to the freedom of the mall, and lined up on them. It was fourteen feet, I knew. How far the sales people were supposed to keep their merchandise from the exit.

Because the trenchcoat man's pistol was a revolver, only had so many bullets, he just held it on each person who escaped and fake shot them, the barrel rising with the sound his mouth was making.

The last of the shoppers to slide under the door on their stomachs wasn't a shopper at all, either. It was Marco.

He splashed through the fountain, silver and copper rising behind him, and was gone.

Trenchcoat man came back to me, scratched his forehead with the sight of his pistol, and said, "You should have gone with him, yeah?"

Story of my life.

Six minutes later—I could tell because my ears were so tuned into the timeclock, which cut the hours into tenths, into six-minutes sections— the trenchcoat man had all of us down on our knees. Not in a single file line, but two single file lines, that crossed where the aisles crossed. From the top of the escalator, that's what we had to be, too: a cross.

It wasn't accidental.

When the bottom of the cross, the base where I was, had needed a little more length, the trenchcoat man had scared up two more bodies from Misses. One of them was Jeanine. Her fists were balled tight, her skin glistening.

I put my hand on her shoulder and the trenchcoat man smiled, nodded me on.

"Get some," he said. "It's the end of the world, man. For you I mean."

I lowered my hand.

When the trenchcoat man had passed, was inspecting his work, how even we were, how much like dominoes, Jeanine shook her head no to him. Said, "It doesn't matter what you do to us, y'know? It won't be as bad as what you'll have waiting for you."

The trenchcoat man nodded, smiled a gap-toothed smile at her, and produced a bible from his right pocket. Waggled it like a revival preacher.

"Talking about this?" he said, stepping in.

Jeanine just stared at him.

"Thou shalt not kill," she said, her voice so even now I thought maybe she was channeling or something. Possessed.

I could feel myself pulling away from her, from the line of fire.

The trenchcoat man leaned down to her, to her ear, his eyes locked on mine, to keep me in place.

"You're right about that, missy," he said. "But you forgot one, too."

She angled her body away enough to face him.

He nodded, opened the bible. Cut into the pages was a box. In the box was a small automatic pistol.

"Why are you doing this?" Jeanine said, shaking her head at him, in disgust.

"Me?" he said back, doing some fake-offended shuffle, then stopping, looking down the line at the rest of us. "More like you, I'd say."

Jeanine held his eyes for maybe three breaths, then turned forward as if he weren't there at all, and started praying.

The trenchcoat man nodded, fingered the gum from his mouth, and fell into Jeanine's prayer with her. Knew it as well as she did.

It shut her up.

He trailed off as well, then held the automatic in front of her, for all of us, and loaded a single shell in, pulled the slide back.

"Don't give it to me," Jeanine said. "I don't want to go to hell for shooting you."

The trenchcoat man shrugged, stared at her, then said, "You're part right, anyway."

It made Jeanine turn to him.

"You are going to hell," he clarified. "But not for me. No. Thou shalt not kill, right? But there's another one. Kind of an automatic deal, like. Don't pass go."

Jeanine smiled now, said it: "Suicide."

Yes.

She closed her eyes, opened them again. Said, "You mean, you're going to hold one gun *on* me, so I'll *shoot* myself? And your threat is that, if I don't shoot myself, then *you* go to hell?"

The trenchcoat man just stared at her.

Jeanine shrugged, held her hand out. Said, "So give it to me then."

This made the man smile, look down the line at the rest of us. To see if we were getting it, if we could see the joke here.

When we couldn't, he pulled the punchline out from behind the counter.

An eight-year-old boy. The pistol to his head.

"Now what do you say?" the trenchcoat man said, and slid the automatic over to Jeanine.

"You don't pick it up," he said, "bang, I go to hell, he goes the other direction. You point it at me...bang. Get it? Make sense?"

Behind us, Gale lost it again, started sobbing, having some sort of attack.

The trenchcoat man sneered at her, pushed the barrel of his chrome pistol deeper into the boy's blond hair.

Outside now, sirens. And Marco, probably still running.

Inside, us, on our knees, in the form of a cross.

It's the best way to be when Jesus comes down from Lingerie.

As you would expect, Jesus wasn't one of those people who walked down the already-moving escalator. Maybe because of his robes, or the sandals he had to have just lifted. It made him look like he was floating, anyway, the way he didn't use the rubber banister. His eyes locked on each of ours in turn, his face so—there's no other word—*serene*.

The trenchcoat man watched him descend too, swallowed whatever he'd had in his mouth.

From somewhere in Mens Casual, a man threw a package of dress socks up against the tile ceiling, to herald Jesus's arrival. The plastic of the sock bag clung to the rough ceiling for three impossible seconds, then the socks tumbled back down in what felt like slow motion, made no sound when they hit the carpet.

Jesus smiled about it, as if in thanks, then folded his arms the way people do in the bible: with his hands up his own wide sleeves.

The teeth at the bottom of the escalator were nothing to him. The whole world.

Instead of keeping to the wide aisle, he navigated through the rounders and t-bars, looking at each of them in turn, finally touching them as he passed, leaving the palm of his hand on them long enough that I knew they were holy now. Cured. Blessed.

I was crying maybe, I don't know.

Jesus fixed the trenchcoat man in his benevolent stare and held him there, turning the pages of his soul, reading the book of his life. When he was done, he nodded, looked down to us again, the corners of his mouth ghosting up a little at me, in recognition. And forgiveness. Then he came back to the trenchcoat man. Said, "You're sure you don't want to reconsider?"

The trenchcoat moved his mouth but didn't have any words.

Oblivious of the chrome pistol, Jesus stepped in, close to the trenchcoat man, then lowered himself to one knee. Not to wash the man's combat boots, but to pick up the cored bible.

"You know why they put my words in red in here?" he said, paging through, amused. He shrugged, looked up to the trenchcoat man. "Supposed to be like blood," he said. "As in, this is my body, this is my—?"

The trenchcoat man gave one nervous nod.

Jesus shut the bible. "I can see you believe," he said, tracing the cross we were all arranged in.

The trenchcoat man nodded again.

Jesus nodded with him, chewed his cheek some. Didn't need to have the ridiculous who-was-going-to-hell-for-what thing explained to him. The way the trenchcoat man was clinging to the eight-year-old boy, the whole scheme was obvious. Undeniable.

"Would you do it?" Jesus said then, focusing in on Jeanine suddenly, intensely. "Would you sacrifice your eternal soul to the save this boy you don't even know?"

Jeanine closed her eyes, nodded. Was crying now.

Jesus looked up to the trenchcoat man and smiled, satisfied. Did something vulgar with his eyebrows it seemed, then shrugged the temptation off. Raised his hand to his beard instead, a tic the bible never said anything about.

Finally, to the trenchcoat man, he said, "You were going to let her do it, too, am I right? Let her make that sacrifice?"

In reply, the trenchcoat man flared his eyes and his nostrils both, and took a long step back. Pushed the barrel of his pistol even harder against the side of the boy's head.

Jesus nodded as if to himself, didn't press the trenchcoat man about it anymore. Said instead, looking back across the store, as if savoring it, "Good thing I showed up then," then came back to the trenchcoat man all at once. "Sacrifice is kind of my thing, y'know?"

Somewhere in her sobs, Jeanine was laughing too now. With joy.

She couldn't see what I could, though: Jesus, lowering himself to the loaded automatic, weighing it in his hands.

"I'm here to take your place," he said to Jeanine, then, looking along the line, at each of us. "All of your places. This sin, what he's asking, it's…it's too much for you. And anyway"—winking once at the eight-year-old—"Jesus loves the little children, right?"

The boy nodded and Jesus liked it, bobbed his head forward as if it was time, now. No more stalling.

He raised the automatic to chest level, held it sideways to study it, the trenchcoat man stepping back again, into a rack of blouses, his eyes all over Jesus's automatic.

Jesus smiled.

"Don't worry," he said, and lifted his face as if hearing something, focused again over the tops of all the clothes, all the merchandise. At the cage bars over the mall entrance, it seemed.

He nodded, shrugged. Said it again, to himself now: "…if there were just one person, willing to take all that sin upon himself…"

He was talking himself into it.

I opened my mouth when I understood, turned all the way around to him, to Jesus, and was too late one more time: already, at the right arm of the cross, Jesus was lowering the small automatic to Gale's left temple.

He didn't close his eyes when he fired, then held the automatic there until Gale had slumped down.

"One," he said, holding his hand back to the trenchcoat man, for another shell. He thumbed it in like it was second nature.

Next was a shopper, still gripping her bag, then another shopper, then up the post part of the cross for Delaney. By this time I wasn't even hearing the small, wet popping sounds anymore. Just Jesus, killing us so we wouldn't have to kill ourselves. Saving our souls, becoming a murderer himself so we wouldn't have to.

Jeanine, singing quietly, perfectly. A hymn, it sounded like. I hummed along as best I could, felt the woman behind me lean forward into my back, dead weight, and closed my eyes for what was coming, what was here, even felt the hot barrel hiss into my hair, and then the shot, the sound, filling the store years before I was ready.

The automatic jerked down to my ear, then my neck, leaving burns in both places, and I turned to see: Jesus was still standing over me, but the center of his robe was red, and spreading.

Opposite his chest, a hundred and fifty feet away, was the mall entrance, the wall of aluminum bars. Resting at shoulder-level on one of those bars the thick barrel of a sniper rifle.

Before Jesus could even fall, the trenchcoat man was dead too, the eight-year-old boy just standing there.

I started to stand, to help him, to shield him—I was *security*, for Chrissakes—but then Jesus was slumping over me, pushing me down, the smell of his hairspray harsh against the back of my throat, his blood washing over me.

From the second floor, Lingerie, we would have been the bottom of the cross, where it's buried in the ground.

I closed my eyes, saw the silk and satin of the teddies up there undulate away from something huge, moving among them. Saw them undulate away and then reach out, after it.

Four months later, I said my first cuss word since the shooting. It was *goddamn*. One of the bad ones.

"Lord's name in vain," Jeanine ticked off for me.

We were in the food court, trying to reclaim our lives.

I slung my finger back and forth where the napkin dispenser had snagged it, said it again: "God-*damn*it, I mean."

Jeanine leaned back in her waffle chair, raised the straw of her red ice drink to her lips. Didn't approve.

Because the sex we'd had two weeks after the shooting had been premarital, and kind of just compulsive, and had started with her explaining the bible to me anyway, she was pretending it had never happened. Repressing me. A mental virgin.

I didn't care.

She wasn't pregnant, I knew, but I was. Not just with the halfway disappointing memory of her breasts, but with something else, something not quite religion, or faith, but having to do with how Jesus' name turned out to be Harold Gaines. How, in those last moments before he started shooting, he, Harold Gaines, had looked across the store to the mall entrance, what was waiting for him, and then done it anyway, lowered the automatic to Gale's head.

How, because of that, I think, I had tried to stand, to save that eight-year-old boy.

How, eight months after signing on, I had become security.

Because Jeanine was still watching me, waiting for me to apologize for breaking the third commandment or eighth amendment or whatever the hell it was, I looked away, over her shoulder. Focused on the shape walking up to our table from the pizza place after four months gone.

It was Marco.

For the briefest possible moment our eyes locked, and I read the pages of what he was here for—his old job, how I could get it for him, because I was a hero, how it would be just like old times—and then I lowered my face. For once in my life did something in the moment, instead of just after: stood, turned, and walked back to the store.

The Salt Angel

Okla Elliott

My eight-year-old niece
does her math homework
at the kitchen table
as I read a German theologian
in a chair by the Christmas tree.
The salt angel
keeps watch over us.
Gritty and translucent is its soul,
bitter and multipurpose.
I close my eyes to concentrate
on a difficult idea
but transition to prayer.
Salt angel, my voice says in my mind,
let this world be kind to us,
her especially.
I open my eyes, see my niece smiling
at me for no reason, smile back,
and return to my reading.

Nocturne: *Crow & Weasel*

Lee Rossi

—*for MS*

All afternoon we lay naked in bed
drinking wine and reading
a children's book to one another,
passing it back & forth like a joint.

Somewhere in our apartment building a TV
blared like the froth & ebb of a storm.
Two boys leave their home in an immense
grass sea. Together they discover forests,

mountains, great rivers and lakes, and people
like themselves, afraid of every stranger.
Wind rattled the bedroom windows,
our voices quavering with glass vibrato.

All summer they travel north
until they come to water so wide
there is no crossing, the bears
great white blocks of ice, the people

so different they forget to be afraid.
Rain pattered like birds flocking on the roof.
And so they returned, and we with them,
having opened the book of wonder,

through snow-drenched passes, bitter valleys,
and rivers of brittle ice, winter passages
and pages of hunger, almost freezing
to death in an ocean of icy grass,

warmth only in the twining
of their own frail bodies.
It doesn't matter who saved them.
God is generous to the young

and quickly shuts the book of suffering.
And then, because we were tired, we made love
and slept in a drift of pillows and sheets,
awaking to darkness and hunger, but lingering

awhile. I caressed her black plumage.
She smoothed my sable fur.
And we listened to the thunder
of closets slamming and closing gates,

as the vastness of our separate lives
opened around us on this,
the last afternoon of childhood.

Idaho Surprise

first published in *Volume III, Issue II*

Julie Weston

Txomin watched the sky change from pale morning blue to the dense graywhite that carried snow. When he first smelled the steely scent, he whistled for his dog.

"Bring 'em down, Baltza." He made a circular motion with his hand. "Curl 'em around the wagon."

Baltza barked and loped around the sheep, pushing and pulling them toward Txomin. They could range again in the morning if the storm blew over, but it wouldn't. Txomin's elbows ached, a sure sign. A dust cloud, filled with the smell of wool oil and trampled sage, swirled in a storm of its own above the sheep.

By dusk, Txomin saw the tell-tale signs when he looked up the canyon. A peak hovered beyond the cloud veil like a spirit. Time to feed the horse and Baltza, get the fire going inside his camp, the covered wagon that had been his home since June. While he grained Blade, the first pellets floated in the air, round and hard. The white balls rolled and piled in the thistle cups, bounced off the dirty white tin roof on the bentwood half cylinder frame of his wagon. They sifted past the door when he opened it to duck through.

Baltza crowded between Txomin's legs and crawled to the edge of the bunk, avoiding Txomin's eyes, pretending to be invisible. His bristled black and brown coat was speckled with white. When Txomin turned to close his door, something moved outside in the fading light, something blue, blending into the twilight. Was it his imagination? A trick of shadow? At that time of day, all of nature seemed blue, ranging from the dense blue of the forest packed solid with firs on the north side of the mountain, to the lavender blue of the sagebrush, fading to distant blue in the mountains on the horizon. Then all the blues shaded into gray, melting in the falling snow. Txomin wasn't even certain he'd seen anything. He stuffed wood into the stove, crinkled an old newspaper page, and lit the fire.

Soon lamb stew filled the cramped space with savory steam. Txomin shook the pan, scraped the gravy from the sides, added more garlic and a half cup of red wine. Stew, thick-crusted bread, and snow. Things could be worse. He could be back at the cabin outside of Shoshone, listening to his grandmother mumble in her sleep, his brother cough and trade insults with his wife, their children whine. Or he could be back on the streets of Bizkaia in Spain, wondering where he would sleep, how he would warm himself.

His old grandmother's letters had pulled him from Spain where he begged money, cigarettes, wine. She demanded he join the family, take up the duties his older brother couldn't perform because of his sickness. Take over the family. Even the wife? Txomin had wondered. That dusky woman with tired eyes, cheeks and lips pulled down by gravity, and who once spoke softly to him when he climbed into the truck with the sheep, on his way to summer range. "Txomin, have a care. Let the desert have its way." He hadn't known what she meant, then.

Hadn't his brother told him: "I only do this for grandmother, wine for brains."

"Eat your sheep," Txomin answered. At first, he refused to be a sheephand, stinking like wool and shit.

"You think you don't stink? Wine and vomit stink. You take the sheep or leave. I got you into America as a Basque sheepherder. If you don't work..." His brother shrugged fat shoulders and coughed. Txomin went.

His camp was three strides long, one-and-a-half wide. When he finished eating, he left his plate on the floor for Baltza and opened the door for snow to wash his cup. In the kerosene lamplight, he saw the pellets had changed to flakes—large feathers thickening, deepening. He would have to stay awake. The sheep could suffocate if they crowded on top of one another to stay warm.

Coffee would help. He threw a cup of grounds into the black dented pan, added creek water from a bottle, shoved more wood into the stove and waited, stretched out on his back in the bunk that filled the end of the wagon, until the water boiled. The burnt toast smell told him when the coffee was ready.

"Baltza, we have to check the sheep. You go."

A quiet whine answered Txomin.

"I went last time. Your turn." Txomin dropped his hand and scratched the dog's ears. Baltza wriggled closer to the bunk, rubbing against the drawer that held Txomin's supplies: the stewpot, a change of jeans, the red flannel shirt, the long canvas coat, the boot oil and saddle soap, a horse blanket, the dog food, his plate, cup, fork and knife, a roll of toilet paper, a shotgun and shells, an extra pair of sox, long underwear, a wool scarf.

"All right, I'll go. You're an old dog, older than me. If I'm 40, you must be 80."

Baltza snuffled and licked Txomin's hand.

"You'll come with me? OK, *zaharra*, old man." Txomin swung his legs around and poured coffee for himself. Snow. From the windows of his grandmother's cabin in the early spring, the snow had looked like pillows in the meadow. From the small window in the door of his sheep camp, the snow looked like death, cold as marble, thick, an expanse of white sand sucking at his sheep, his horse, his dog, him.

"It's only a September storm, Baltza. Gone in a day, two at the most." Txomin pulled the flaps of his hat over his ears, shrugged on his coat, smoothed on his sheepskin gloves, picked up the lamp. A liniment rub by his old grandmother was what he wished for.

Outside, intricate crystals whirled in a kaleidoscopic pattern around the bright flame, sizzling into steam when they touched the glass, and wetting the skin of his cheek, clinging to the dog's whiskers. The world was white and black.

"Come, Baltza. We have work to do." Txomin heard the upbeat of his own voice because he didn't have to sit doing nothing all evening. Loneliness dulled the time, made each minute last an hour. Two-and-a-half months in the high desert and mountains had passed; only three weeks to go. Then he could leave the sheep, leave his brother and return to Spain with money in his pocket. His grandmother had promised.

So far, so good. The sheep clustered, but not in the tight knots that warned of panic. Baltza circled the band and returned to Txomin. An hour later, they checked again. This time, Baltza didn't return. His bark, sharp above a wind beginning to quarrel with the aspens, told Txomin that his dog was bringing back strays.

Txomin didn't like the wind. He thought of mounting Blade to check down the canyon, see how far the corral was. He'd left it last spring in a gully-washer when he barely saved the lambs, and he needed to get some bearings. This storm could be an Idaho surprise, not just a quick flurry. But it was too dark. He wouldn't see the castle rock he remembered, nor the twist in the canyon bottom where the fresh green sage had been ripped away by the spring gusher.

What to do? The temperature was dropping again. Moisture on his mustache from the coffee and perspiration in the creases of his neck from the heat in the wagon had frozen. He left Blade tied to the back of the wagon, retrieved the horse blanket and covered his horse's haunches. "Maybe I should try and take you inside, Blade." He rubbed the white diamond on Blade's muzzle. "I could fit you out with a diaper so you wouldn't shit in there." Txomin loosened the rope. "Nah." What was he thinking of? The animal's two front legs, maybe. He tied Blade once more to the rear. The horse rested his long face on Txomin's shoulder, then whinnied.

Txomin whistled. The shrill sound seemed to bounce off the snowflakes and fall in a slurp to the ground. He cupped his hand around his mouth. "Baltza!"

A sheep bawled, then another. Txomin lifted the lamp and a halo formed. Sheep were beginning to huddle near the wagon, pushing at each other, bleating in nervous harmony. He whistled again, a two-level signal, his and Baltza's own code for trouble. Coyotes, maybe, were spooking the woollies. No wolves around. They'd been introduced into Yellowstone—miles away from the grass gullies and canyons riddling the back country above the Stanley Basin.

Coyotes, he could handle, unless a pack formed. The only ones he'd seen when he moved the sheep from range to range had traveled alone or sometimes with one companion, their long snouts and ribbed bodies looking lean and hungry. No excuse for that—there were plenty of voles, squirrels, chipmunks, field mice, and even beavers along some of the creeks that flowed into the Salmon River.

Txomin hadn't lost a sheep all summer, not even in the fire that threatened the high feeding ground in August. He didn't intend to start now. That would give his brother an excuse not to pay him. Old grandmother could protect Txomin from most of his brother's abuses, but not that one, not if he lost a portion of the band. Resentment warmed him, and then he remembered Baltza.

From the wagon, Txomin picked up the battered gun, a pocketful of shells, and, grabbing his lantern again, stepped back into the storm. His legs pushed through the milling sheep. He talked to them quietly, "Home range you go soon, you woolly *txoriburu*, idiots. Hush hush. Txomin won't let the coyotes eat you."

His brother's image floated in the light's shadow—sagging jowls, broken nose, stringy black hair with gray streaks. He remembered the wheezing cough. Sometimes at night in the crowded cabin, the wheeze hesitated. Txomin could feel everyone draw in a breath and hold it. Would his brother choke this time?

No one else would take the sheep to the high country and live alone three or four months of the year—away from women, *txakoli*, family. Alone with stars, white sun, dusty sage, flies—always flies, rocky mountains, and wind, wind, wind, until he thought he'd go mad if he didn't jump into it and sail away. Alone with himself, to think about his hands shaking from drink, his lost jobs—road worker, janitor, lottery ticket seller—his sweet *neska* who married another, his putrid mouth in the morning, his shame before his grandmother. Some nights, he was so alone, he crawled outside the wagon, rolled naked in sage and dust until dirt and scratches ran with blood and he knew he was still alive.

"Baltza, let me hear you!"

Txomin listened. A snarl and then a bark filled the spaces between the flakes. He sidestepped free of the sheep and found himself wading in snow as high as his knees in places. Drifting snow. Coyotes. Baltza maybe wounded, fighting for his life. Txomin hung the lantern on his arm near his elbow and dragged two shells from his pocket, clicked them into the opened breech of the gun, and snapped it closed, the way his brother had showed him. He'd never shot anything before.

He pulled his neck in, letting his coat cover the lower half of his face. Moisture from breathing dampened the collar, freezing it against his lower lip, but he had the illusion of warmth when his breath expelled from his mouth. Each step carried him into unknown space, away from his wagon and his horse. Snow cascaded from his boots. This snow didn't crunch and creak; it sifted, filling the boot hole like silt as soon as his leg lifted and swung forward. His tracks would disappear before he could retrace them. Fear rattled, coiled and waiting like a summer snake in his city-boy gut.

At the farthest edge of the sheep band, blood patches appeared black in the lamplight. A sheep? Baltza? The snow was sculptured in swirls and humps; a portion was tramped flat. Under the lamp, a trail of blood marked a deep groove, as if a broom had swept along the hillside between clumps of sage and across the snow. One sheep, two, even three, but not Baltza. He needed Baltza.

With lantern held high, Txomin strained to peer beyond the blowing snow. Light reflected off the sheeps' eyes, twin gold spots here, there, staring at him, like cats' eyes. A long howl rose on mournful notes and then trailed into the wind. His hackles stirred. He remembered the shadow at dusk, the blue ghost. The night paused. Txomin thought he could hear each snowflake whisper as it landed. Then yips sang into the night—coyotes. He could deal with coyotes.

Barks in the distance, fading. Baltza was in trouble. Why did he leave the band? He wouldn't do that unless he was protecting a straggler. At supper the sheep had seemed secure, close to the wagon. Maybe a mountain lion, scarce as they had become in Idaho, had crept from the heights and found his sheep, cut one out for itself and murdered the peace.

When he tried to move faster, Txomin slipped sideways. He should have ridden Blade. Instead, he had picked up the lantern and begun his climb, forgetting his scarf, not stopping to plan, acting first, acting dumb. Just like his brother said.

In the first month, Txomin had drunk half the summer's wine supply and let the dog work while he slept most of the day in the shade. He lost Blade twice, turned his ankle and cut his arm on a rock when he fell off the top of the wagon, begged the supply man to take his place. One night, Txomin had stumbled from the wagon, screaming at the moon, "I hate you." He fell on his face, sobbing and dripping tears and snot into the dirt.

Hate who? If he expected the *Guardia Civil* to kick him, beat him, and at last throw him in jail for a week or two to sober up, he was in the wrong place. Baltza had circled Txomin, pushing at his legs, nosing his arms and neck and hand. A dog, a stupid animal. But Baltza did his job, kept the sheep rounded up, ate his food, slept, scissored his legs in dreams on the wagon floor, woke and did his job again. That's all Txomin had to do: keep the sheep together and safe, eat, sleep, dream. Could he do that? Could he do as much as Baltza did?

Txomin had rolled over, grabbed Baltza's black head and held it with both hands, touching his nose to the dog's. Soft, cool, grainy damp touching his own dry skin, his own running nose. "Baltza, you tell me. I'll do it."

The dog, named for his dark color, had scrambled to his feet, shaken himself, and trotted off to the sheep. Since then, Txomin talked to Baltza, and Baltza talked to Txomin. When Txomin thought he'd go crazy listening to his own voice and the flies droning in the summer heat, hearing the rumbles in his head or the click of rain and hail on the tin roof, he climbed up to his sheep. Followed Baltza around the band, cradling his thoughts in the bleats, finding words for what they said to each other. "Baa: Grass, green. Baaa: Water, wet."

In the canyon, Txomin waded as best he could. The sheep were behind him. He was alone when the ghost crept from the shadows into the circle of his lamplight. A wolf. Big across the shoulders, pale eyes staring at Txomin, his tail flat, his fur light gray but silvered on the tips, almost blue. The gun felt heavy in Txomin's arms. Could he lift and fire it before the wolf lunged at his neck, punctured his artery, shook his body and dragged it to his pack? All the stories he'd heard since he came to sheep country echoed in his head. 'Bloodthirsty killer,' 'cruel,' 'child-nabber,' 'murderer.'

The coyotes yelped again. A whimper followed. Baltza! Txomin lifted his gun. The wolf's mouth grinned open; sharp incisors reflected light. His pink and wet tongue panted. He turned and began to lope slowly toward the racket. Txomin lowered his gun and jogged after it, staying in the path cleared by the dead animal. He couldn't trot as fast as the wolf, but the wolf stopped to sniff the air when Txomin tripped or fell behind.

They came to a flat meadow. The snow had stopped and the clouds began to part, letting moonlight pour through. Four coyotes pulled and jerked at the innards of a fallen sheep, feasting and growling their greed. Two of them faced Baltza, who jumped toward them, then away. One of the coyotes leaped at the dog's throat. They rolled and snarled in the snow, thrashing and growling, tangling their legs. Txomin dropped his lantern and raised his gun, but he couldn't fire. He'd kill his dog along with the coyote.

The wolf howled, a high keen. Like a frieze of jackals, all the animals ceased their motion and faced the wolf and Txomin. Baltza barked. The wolf coiled itself and sprang at the coyotes standing over the sheep. He bit the shoulder of the nearest. The others hesitated a moment, then ran, streaming away in the dark. The wolf stalked the pack, leaving the wounded coyote. Baltza looked at Txomin, then at the wild animals. He took one step, two. The lamp sputtered and failed, and a cloud crossed the moon. Black gripped Txomin and his fear uncoiled. Fear of the blood, the coyotes, the ghost, the lonely hole of night. Here in the snow he would die.

Out of the darkness, he felt rather than saw the body hurtle at him—long, skinny, claws and jaw pointed at his neck. Eighty pounds landed on him, knocking him against the useless lamp, flailing him into the snow, down, black, kicking, yipping, shouting, white, barking, rolling over and over.

"You old son-of-a-bitch!" Txomin snuggled his face in the cold bristles and against the bony head. His dog's tongue licked Txomin's lips, his cheeks, his forehead and his eyes, until he could feel the saliva freeze. They lay still, their chests chuffing and mingling steam.

"Are you hurt?"

Baltza answered in short bursts, then jumped free and tried to lead Txomin up the hill.

"No. I cannot come, old man. My lamp is out."

His dog circled and yipped, dashing once toward the fallen sheep, then back to Txomin.

"Yeah, I know. A sheep is dead. Not your fault."

Baltza whined.

"It's okay. I'll explain. The wolf can have it. Let's get back to the camp."

The last word settled Baltza. He pressed against Txomin's leg, and led the sheepherder down the steep pitch of the canyon, through the sheep, to the camp door.

"Round 'em up again." He circled his hand. "I'll wait. Then we'll have a hot one."

Baltza and this band belonged to Txomin, maybe not by law, but by experience. A peculiar feeling, close to exaltation, seeped into him. They'd escaped a flash flood down Boundary Creek in June. They'd suffered the high heat days in July, a prairie fire in August, and all the long, lonely days in between. And he and Baltza and most of the sheep had survived a snowstorm in September.

The sheep settled, huddling close to each other, looking like the mounds of yarn his grandmother stored in a basket near her chair. When the dog returned, Txomin scratched one of his ears, then opened the wagon door. A mixture of garlic, coffee, and waning heat brushed their noses. "What do you say? Think we could survive another summer?" Txomin pulled off his hat, slapped it against his thigh, and said: "After you, *señor*."

Sensitive Habitat Area, Hwy 43

Don Thompson

Scattered steers move solemnly
through the amber grass,
ignoring it—well-fed or not.
Less like meat on the hoof
than Franciscans in brown habits,
muttering prayers
from the ruminants' breviary,
they stop now and then and look up,
the way we do, listening
to the articulate silence
that answers them.

Days After

first published in *Volume IX*

Patricia Colleen Murphy

For me it is a time for more horses.
Mane-hair bleached at the tips,
eyes bowled and glassy,
noses fleshy, mottled, low.

From this comes a bulbous anger,
some noxious desire,
some unspeakable marriage
between what is present or is not.

Some days it is as easy as
cushioning my own dark weight.
Beyond the city limits
ten thousand moons crest and fall.

The last time I saw you alive
the night had just cut its own teeth.

So now I am left to this:
Some solemn wandering.
Some structured
mounting of offenses.

Ukiyo-e

Robert Kostuck

Hokkaido recreates itself: my memory fills in the blanks. Brown shorelines and chalk scribble clouds, lemon crescent moons and zigzag rivers, streaks of wiry grass and fields that follow contours of the land. Fantastic landscapes, Edo period artwork, Ukiyo-e, *Pictures of the Floating World*, Hiroshige, Utamaro, Hokusai: famous artists of the past. I learned a little bit about 18th century wood block prints in college. In North Carolina, I learned how Americans love them because they think of them as pre-photography photographs. In this dream world, rain is a fifth season woven throughout the year, a single human figure in a plain kimono leans into it while crossing a bridge.

I never outgrew my childhood manga and anime obsessions— just replaced them with a computer geek lifestyle. My nose quite literally in a coding book, and I am easy prey for hungry men, which my mother did not prepare me for.

A national forest wraps around Haboro; my hometown looks out to sea. The air is pure oxygen, the colors navy blue and hunter green. I'm the only passenger to step down from the bus. No one greets me. Tourist attractions staggered on both sides of the Ororon Line; the Sunset Plaza Hotel still reminds me of a futuristic spaceship. Everything in my old neighborhood looks smaller.

The first morning our home is empty of sound. Like me, my little sister Kumiko left long ago. Mother and father are older, slower.

Grandmother looks the same. The house creaks. My father retired from his job at the bank, and now my parents circle photographs in seed catalogues and discuss the merits of goat manure. The enclosed yard is now wall-to-wall garden. I slip into the new rhythms, help mother shovel dirt and fork compost, help father plan meals. Sorrow withers in the sunlight.

"Keiko-chan, you are a beautiful woman," says mother. "And you know so much about the world now. We thought you would marry and stay in Carolina. Cape Hatteras, I looked it up on the Internet, an island in the ocean. The photographs you posted on your blog. It reminded you of home?"

"Chapel Hill is far from the ocean," I say. "I only went to the coast when I had a long weekend. It's a five hour drive. You read my blog?"

"Is this a vacation?"

"For now."

"Your shape is different," says my mother. "You were always so skinny."

"We all get old."

"Did you have a baby?"

"Ma! What kind of question is that? Are you crazy?"

"Do not say I'm crazy, young lady; show respect! You lived with that man for so long. No children?"

"Obviously I have no children, did you see me arrive here with any children? And I was never pregnant. I was never even married. How can you ask such a thing?"

"Is it so different in America?" she says. "I prayed that you would marry."

"No children, never pregnant, never married. Andy and I split up and went our own ways months ago. We were both headed in dif-

"Pfft!" She laughs. "You need someone to cook your meals and wash your socks."

After the introductions Shigeru shares a secret. He punctuates his fast, rural dialect with slang.

"I learned to fish the old way, by the color of the water, by the movement of the birds. So, I go where the others say there is nothing, and I always get what I want. Plus, I feed the spirits that guide the fish. They are especially partial to rice or soba noodles soaked in tamari."

"You drop food in the water?" I say. "Isn't that superstitious?"

My grandmother elbows me. "Hey!"

"Call it whatever you want," he says, "it works."

"I missed something," I say. "Did you say dōkutsu? I don't remember any caves on this coast."

He pokes a dead fish with a gaffing hook.

"Not on the coast. Under the water. I've never seen them but I've pulled up crab and octopus pots that were torn apart. Even strong currents won't do that." He pats the girl's head. "But, I don't want to scare Misaki."

We buy his fish; stop to purchase canned goods and a ten-kilo bag of rice.

"What an interesting man," I say. "Offering food to the sea spirits."

"I've known him for years," says grandmother.

On Sunday we walk to the edge where village meets sea. Grandmother directs me to a tall hedge with a solid wood gate painted calm-summer-ocean blue. Sweet smoke trickles from a window. She stares at faded characters on the lintel.

"I don't remember this house at all," I say.

"It has always been here," she says. "It was old before you were born."

On the way to the jetty I offer Misaki my hand but she ignores me. Shigeru walks beside my grandmother

"Sachiko," he says, "you are still the most beautiful woman in the world."

She ignores him, rolls up her trouser legs, and wades into the cold shallows. He lights a cigarette and follows, gestures to the girl to stay. Two elders stand alongside the boat, talking, running hands across planks.

"The water here is so blue," I say. "Let's go in?"

"No way," says Misaki.

"How old are you?"

"Twelve."

"Well, Misaki, my name is Keiko. I like you and I want to be your friend. I don't feel like getting wet right now, either. You want to go look for seashells?"

The beach is sand and shell fragments, and occasional whole, polished shells: brown, amber, purple, pink, white, black; completely different from the shells of North Carolina's Atlantic coast.

"Look what I found." She pokes a dead crab with a stick. "Touch it. I dare you."

I pick it up with my fingertips and my stomach churns. "Eww, we can't eat that. We need fresh fish that your grandfather catches."

"The níngyo will eat this." She takes the crab from me, throws it into the rushing waves.

"Níngyo?" I say. "Do they live around here?"

She pulls her arm against her chest.

"Way far out in the ocean and way down at the bottom, in a cave with broken glass and green lights. The cave is full of skeletons of people and fish. They're monsters. They bite people and eat them. It's how they stay young. When a storm comes and the waves are big, they come to the top of the water. They scratch at the bottom of the boat."

"How do you know all this?"

"My grandfather told me some of it," she says. "Most of it I dreamed. That was last year when my arm was still bandaged. When it happened it scared my mom and dad. They freaked out. There's an anime about them, but it's all wrong. They're more fish than person."

"What about today?" I say. "Will they come today?"

"No, not today. Maybe I shouldn't have thrown that crab in the water. That's bad luck."

"You're not going in, are you?"

"I never go the sea anymore," she says.

We return to the house with the blue gate. A woman's wail cuts the afternoon light.

"That's my mom," says Misaki. "She prays a lot. She's not herself, so please don't worry about being polite. Her name's Emiko."

I greet the child's father inside the door.

"Finally," he says to Misaki. "Go to your mother before she loses her voice."

We open the door and the shrill petition stops. Incense smolders in a dish of sand. Smoke curls through a tangle of fresh cut flowers. A fragile cup with a chrysanthemum pattern, a thin film of ash on the stale saki. Emiko kneels before the shrine, hands on her narrow legs, waiting. We are about the same age.

"Mom, I'm home." She hugs her mother. "Hey, I'm back. Look up Mom. This is Keiko-san. She didn't go in the water either. We got some shells instead."

Emiko raises her head without turning around.

"I've been thinking, Misaki-chan. There're worse things than what happened. They lure and trick you into eating their flesh; they trick you into becoming one of them. I'm telling you this—Shigeru and his fish—who knows what could happen? Now you must be careful about what you eat. That's how it happens, you know. The níngyo need companions or they die of loneliness. It's the only thing that kills them." She turns to me, stares pointedly at my flat torso, and inside, a womb that never took seed. "Thank you for watching over my daughter."

"Daddy and I will make dinner again tonight," says Misaki. "You should sleep for a while, okay?" We leave her to her prayers.

"I grew up here," I say. "You're going to the same high school I attended."

"Are you going to live here now?" says Misaki.

"I guess so. I really don't have anywhere else to go."

"Will you come see me again?"

"My mother saved my collection of manga books," I say. "You come see me."

That night there is a new moon. Alone in the room of my childhood, I flip and sweat on a dry futon, review my mother's sly comments about unmarried women, reflect how that fact has nothing to do with the passage of time, decay of the body, scars that accumulate on the heart. Kumiko and I would lie awake at night in this room, whispering plans for the limitless future. When did age overcome passion and dreams?

Morning is still hours away when I fall asleep. A níngyo comes to me then, enticing me with plaints of loneliness and promises of eternal life. A scarred face, glaucomatous eyes, and an almost lipless mouth—a mask on which is plainly written: retribution and hunger, jealousy and greed.

She takes my hand and flicks her tail. Together we swim into darkness. Three meters of coarse hair trail from her head, a stunted river of cuttlefish ink. Globules of blood stream from the mouth of an underwater cave where dozens of goblin sharks gather and writhe. She tugs me past the sharks and through the narrow entrance. Papery nautilus shells stuffed with phosphorescent algae illuminate a cave lined with mirror shards salvaged from sunken ships. Her sisters take bites from a large flatfish. Seashell tattoos decorate their arms and bare breasts. At the place where their bleached skin changes to scales they wear pearls in their navels. Their language is a dolphin dialect; the subject, food.

The oldest níngyo blinks her one good eye and fights with another. They tear apart a rotted crab, vomit shell fragments, entrails: a snowstorm of debris swirls in the water. Serrated dagger teeth, kelpy hair, missing fingers, torn fins. An insatiate hunger.

"One-Eye is a thousand years old and falling to pieces," says my guide. "She is not eternal." She pulls One-Eye's arm toward me. "One bite and you can live forever."

"So tempting," I say. "To multiply this wasted life."

"Little sister, join us." Her hair tangles my arms and legs, chokes me.

I wake with a quilt twisted around my body. There are no níngyo. Rushing waves recede into early morning thunder. From the edge of the sea a broken woman calls to me in a sing-song voice.

"Mom, do we have any soba noodles?" I say.

"You want noodles for dinner tonight?" says my mother.

"I'm just going to cook some."

"I've made soup."

"Not for my breakfast. They're for a friend."

When the noodles are done, I dump them in a plastic food container and drench them with tamari. In my room, I use a knife to pry the mirror from the inside of the jewelry box, place the mirror on top of the noodles, and seal the container.

I wrap myself in my mother's plain gardening kimono, pop open my father's proper banker's umbrella, and cross empty streets to the house with the blue gate. Emiko greets me, eyes red and tear-stained, a small bundle of incense sticks in one hand.

"You called me back from a mistake I was about to make," I say, "and I thank you. Please give this to Shigeru-san. It's an offering to the sea spirits; to the níngyo. I want them to leave me alone. I want to grow old in my own time."

"Sister," says Emiko. "Pray for our children." She trades the plastic container of food for the bundle of fuming incense.

Trailing smoke, I wander into the fifth season of rain, make my way to the edge where sky and water meet. Earth-tone kimono and black umbrella, I lean aslant against a sharply angled sky, stylized mountains, pine trees, and bobbing fishing boats. Seashells crunch underfoot, the waves reach for my feet.

I cross a bridge and enter the floating world.

Jotted on the Underside

Paulann Petersen

—for my grandmother, Ann Theobald, 1892–1972

Sixteen words, that's all.
One misspelled, two capitalized
for emphasis, two others
each solo on a line.
          In your cursive,
they scrawl across the back
of a black and white Brownie snapshot
taken of you and Nell posed outside,
in your garden.
          A sentence to tell
what Nell said. A fragment to explain
what she meant. An enquiry lacking
a question mark.
          You and your best friend
stand in 40's dresses—black, tailored,
blunt-shouldered. Both of you wear
a hat listing sharp to the right—
left eyes struck by sunshine, rights
swooped into shadow. Rakish,
folks said of you two.

Nell's hat, a dark straw skimmer.
Yours, an even darker pillbox
that sprouts, at your forehead,
a pale silk blossom
big as your fair-skinned face
lifting to the camera.
                    Summer 1948.
Dressed to the nines, you're both wearing
white gloves. The camera's held low
to get a full-length view, to catch—
in the foreground—your garden's
pride, tall white lilies, each stalk
bugling a fanfare of blooms.
You're long dead. Nell too.
Still, I talk to you, Nana,
there in your side yard
standing next to a flower bed
no one has tended in decades.
You answer me, saying
the sixteen words
lying beneath your likeness
alive in that garden.

> *Nell says Here*
> *are the Prettiest*
> *flowers in the*
> *yard. Meaning*
> *us.*
> *Aren't the Lillies*
> *grand.*

Before you fall
silent, you pose your final question—
so sure in your asking,
you choose the mark
to make of it
an anthem.

Dear Darius, Dear Cyrus,

Darius Atefat-Peckham

While looking for my late mother in the chaos of
Her paintings, Bibi insists there is structure,
That's a tulip, you see it? And she
Points at orange and blue
Lines that swirl tightly and crash.

Getting to know my mother
Reminded me of Cyrus's search through playground
Mulch for little girls' hairclips. Later,
He'd gift the colorful molds, lost from
Careless pigtails like gems cradled gently in his
Small hands, his face serious,
Waiting quietly for her smile. It
Was a hunt for Post-It notes
Stuck in between pages of large volumes,
Her scribbles in the margins of
Coffee stained books or letters to
Her first love written in code that
Bibi and I translated with a key that
She had left us, cackling insanely.
She must be laughing at us. Bibi would say,
Wiping away tears. And I would smile sadly.

Yes, she must. Or her daily
Notes to Cyrus that she stuck in his
Lunchbox, all kept neatly in folders.
She'd write to us (brothers then) letters for when we
Grew older. As if she knew what would happen,
Everything was documented.

While weeding through scattered old suitcases
And pocketbooks, her wedding
Gown and emailed condolences, Bibi finds
The baggie of hairclips in her hands and they tremble
As she tells me stories.

Later, I stand in *The Gallery* of my mother's paintings and
Let the back of my knuckles brush
Their texture until I've half-convinced
Myself there is a pattern; Here—
A faint stem branching out into fiery
Petals, and there—
A flower; slowly wilting.

Go Anywhere

Patricia Colleen Murphy

You told me the story of the park ranger
who discovered that overnight a petroglyph
had been excised. She followed the trail rut
to the McMansion of a man who answered
his door dressed in a towel, the stolen rock
well-lit above his mantel. And what is there

to say? I'm certain there are topics about which
I know nothing. I moved from Ohio to this desert
with two suitcases and a poorly laid plan. The first
week I was here I called the landlord to complain
about the dust and he explained monsoons to me.
I thought, *What the hell have I done?*

Decades later I'm bitching my way through triple digits.
If you could go anywhere, where would you go?
You and I can, now, that all four of our parents died.
I thought I'd move to France, maybe lose too much
weight. But I fell in love with you and here we are.

Should we go to the park, help ourselves to free wall art?
Because being here feels like stealing as it is.

Reason's Dance

Zev Torres

Approach cautiously those pesky
    Subterranean reasons

    Nibbling at our moral and
Spiritual infrastructure

Inciting us to act in ways that
    Defy good sense and

    Our long-term prospects
That are more opaque than

Quantum particles engaged
    In their chaotic dance. But

    Do not spurn them altogether
Because chaos often yields

Positive outcomes
    Created in the image of the same

Unintelligible disarray
That gives birth to us all.

Some Extensions on the Sovereignty of Science

first published in *Volume II, Issue II*

Alberto Ríos

—for my father

1.

When the thought came to him it was so simple he shook his head.
People are always looking for kidneys when their kidneys go bad.

But why wait? Why not look when you're healthy? If two good kidneys
Do the trick, wouldn't three do the job even better?

Three kidneys. Maybe two livers. You know. Two hearts of course.
Instead of repairing damage, why not think ahead?

Why not soup up the car? Why not be a touring eight-cylinder classic,
Or one of those old, sixteen-cylinder, half-mile long Duesenbergs?

2.

The hardest work of the last quarter of the 20th century is to find
An edge in the middle. When something explodes, for example,

Nobody is confused about what to do—you look toward it.
Loud is a magnet. But the laws of magnetism are more complex.

One might just as well try this: when something explodes,
Turn exactly opposite from it and see what there is to see.

The loud will take care of itself, and everyone will be able to say
What happened in their direction. But who is looking

The other way? Nature, that magician and author of loud sounds,
Zookeeper and cook, electrician and provocateur—

Maybe these events are Nature's slight of hand, and the real
Thing that's happening is in the other hand,

Or behind or above or inside us.

3.
On a recent trip to Bloomington, Indiana, I was being driven there
From Indianapolis, and my friend along the way pointed out some
        hills,

Saying that these hills were made as a result of the farthest reach of
The Ice Age glacier. I had been waiting for this moment

Ever since fifth grade. I could hardly contain myself,
Though I'm sure I just said *uh-huh* in the conversation.

I took a small and delicious breath. "So," I said, slowly,
"That's the terminal moraine, huh?" There, I'd said it,

The phrase I had saved up since the moment I found it
In that fifth grade reader: "terminal moraine."

I had never said it aloud. What's a little scary, of course,
Is that I was more excited about remembering

Than about the hills themselves. But if it was scary it was sweet
in the mouth too. In a larger picture, one way or the other,

The Ice Age glacier was still a force to be reckoned with.

4.
The reason you can't lose weight later in life is simple enough.
It's because of how so many people you know who have died,

And that you carry a little of each of them with you.

5.
The smallest muscle in the human body is in the ear.
It is also the only muscle that does not have blood vessels;

It has fluid instead. The reason for this is clear:
The ear is so sensitive that the body, if it heard its own pulse,

Would be devastated by the amplification of its own sound.
In this knowledge I sense a great metaphor,

But I do not want to be hasty in trying to capture or describe it.
Words are our weakest hold on the world.

In the Republic of Mud

John Sibley Williams

It was easy once, with so many ships
cutting wakes across the sky, to string
a few stars together and swing out over

the surface of night. Maybe we shouldn't
fossilize all our myths just yet.
This is what I'll tell my children:

let the trees go on believing in their gods.
In yarrow and thistle. This republic of mud.
The inevitability of seed. Of course,

following the map on the underside of a leaf
leads nowhere we haven't already lived;
but I won't tell them

soil crumbles like saints no matter
how hard you squeeze, that no place is home
until someone has died to keep it.

I'll show them how easy it can be
to plant tulips upside down, saying
this is how you brighten hell.

And we will brighten hell. Yes,
the stars will support us even as dawn
bursts them into a million empty mouths.

Offerings

Paulann Petersen

For morning prayer this December day,
I stare at an image of Lord Ganesh,
the elephant-headed god, lover of sweets.
Even his pet rat nibbles on a golden candy
clawed from a mounded bowl.
A flower garland sheds petals
onto his knotted rug.
A five-flamed lamp sets off
its tiara glow.
        I'm too fat already for even
the smallest mountain of sugar.
My North American winter garden scoffs
at swelling buds. The tiara I own
is a joke-gift, cheap sparkler
bought for me from a mall's kiosk
that caters to each princess
of a prom.
        Nowhere in my Episcopal
Book of Common Prayer did a god crave
sweets. On not a single page did a deity
possess more than two arms.

The Virgin Mary was not a goddess.
Our Deacon warned against believing that.
In no prayer did Mary do
what Lakshmi does—one pair
of her goddess hands raised to hold
two blown blooms of lotus.
No words writ Episcopalian
allowed third and fourth arms
to drop along her sides, those palms
open, gold coins flowing
from each.
        That's abundance, not money,
streaming from Lakshmi's fingertips.
The lotus is her many-wicked
flower, sprouting its rosy anther-flames.
Her sari is pure silk, her bangles
precious.
        My *Book of the All Too Common*
was small, bound in black pebbled paper.
Meant to resemble leather, that cover
crumbled under years of my touch.
Little enough, it fit into the slightest of my
childhood hands.
        Are those coins cold
when they emerge on Lakshmi's palms?
Do they cool her fingers as they fall?
At her temple, hands of Lakshmi's devotees
offer—to her jeweled and gilded idol—

folded pieces of tacky spangled cloth
meant to look like priceless saris she might
someday wear.
                    The quarter I clutched
for the church offering dish grew warmer
each minute within my left hand's
lesser grip. Even then, my childhood's
two-bit coin was never
purely silver.
                    At any Temple of Ganesh,
worshippers offer trays mounded
with cheap confections, the priest
sliding them toward Ganesh's huge statue,
so close their rims touch
his plump pink toes.
                    I once stared and stared
at the staked and bleeding feet of Jesus
as he hung on the cross above the altar—
so tendoned, so narrow, so thin.
In another world, I might have offered him
something to ease his anguish.
A sweetmeat.
                    The body of Christ lay
dry and wan on my tongue,
his blood an acrid echo
in my breath.
                    I said my prayers.
My *Most Common Book* sprouted

a thin, black—and surely not silk—
ribbon to make certain

> I kept my place.

The Saved

first published in *Volume V, Issue I*

Joe Hill

Jubal Scott and Drake Hough were at the side of the road a little before noon, holding their shovels but not putting them to any use, when the foreman Tierney came upon them.

"Scott," he said to Jubal. "You better get on now."

"I said I'd wait till three."

Tierney pointed a finger straight up at the low and overcast sky. The bottoms of the heavier looking clouds were streaked with a color like that of fresh-turned earth. Here and there a little round fleck of snow dropped spiraling from above.

"If this starts to stack up, you'll be sorry you waited. Go on. See you Monday."

"Hey, John," said Drake Hough. "I was thinkin' of kickin' off early today too. I got places to go myself."

"Places to go. I'll give you someplace to go. Unemployment line."

Jubal Scott took his shovel with him to his International, parked down the road, and threw the spade *clang* into the flatbed. The International was eight years old and its cost had been a hundred and fifteen dollars; he had purchased it from another man on the crew four months before. Jubal had just finished paying off what was owed on it, and to celebrate he had decided to drive it north to see his daughter Kelly. Jubal and his wife were separated. Linda had gone back to her people in Maine and taken their daughter with her. Jubal hadn't been to see Kelly in going on three years. As the truck bumped up out of the high grass and into the road, Jubal pressed the horn, and a few on the work crew lifted their hats to him.

Jubal ran the truck with the side windows lowered a crack to keep the windshield from fogging over. Air shrieked and whistled through the openings. He huddled in his denim jacket, a watch cap pulled down to the tops of his ears, a blanket over his legs. The International didn't have a heater, and in the cab was a deadening cold. After an hour of driving, the only thing warm was his right foot. The iron pedals pulsed with a low persistent heat, transmitted in some way from the working of the engine. He could feel the warm glow of the iron through the sole of his boot.

He considered for a time what he would say when he arrived on Linda's porch. The first thing he had done, when the idea of this trip had come to him back in October, was write a letter to Linda, to say he planned a visit and hoped he would be welcome. He put five dollars into the envelope with the letter, so Linda would have a good recent memory about him when he appeared on her step.

As he was dropping his letter into the postal box, Jubal felt a moment of disquiet, trying to remember the last time he had sent money. He knew he hadn't in September or August, when it was necessary to use all his extra cash to pay what was owed on the truck. But he thought maybe in July—he had a very clear memory of putting a ten in an envelope, along with something he had found for Kelly, a tail feather from a hawk. At the very worst he had sent money in June, so close to the end of the month it was practically July.

Jubal had promised Linda he would send money as a regular thing, but in truth had not lived up to his promise well. For years, work had been catch as catch can, and he had caught little. He fell so out of the habit of sending money, that when he did come into a job, he sometimes didn't remember for a while to put a few dollars into the mail. He tried not to think too closely about what he had and hadn't done for Linda and Kelly; that kind of thinking made him uneasy and contributed to a lack of sleep. There were, after all, lots of men who would think not a moment about doing nothing.

It was early, but the light was already bad, brownish and dim. It never seemed to really start snowing, but by the time he crossed from New Hampshire into Maine, the macadam was covered in a white film that blew in sideways streams across the road. His face was so cold there was no sensation in it. The cold seemed to reach all the way back into his brain. It was easy to sink into a kind of hollow-headed trance, and drive automatically, with no consciousness at all of what his hands were doing on the wheel, or his right foot was doing among the pedals.

Jubal had settled into this winter trance very deeply when a furious gust of wind roared out of the pines and over the highway and swiped the truck across the side. The gust pushed so hard it drove the truck right to the edge of the road, and for a heart-stopping few moments the tires were catching dirt, spinning up gravel to rattle against the undercarriage, and Jubal was struggling all astonished with the wheel. The wind slackened, and he steered the truck back into the center of his lane. His pulse slammed in his ears, and the sweat on his face was cold and unpleasant. He was grinning a scared grin and didn't know it.

When he saw the man at the side of the highway, ten minutes later, he slowed down and pulled over without a thought. Jubal rolled past him, came to a stop thirty feet beyond, and waited for the hitchhiker to catch up. The man from the side of the road opened the door and pulled himself up and in—his movements awkward, as if his joints were stiff from the chill—and slammed the door.

"Too cold to walk," Jubal said. "Your ass must be froze."

"Yes, sir. I thank Jesus you picked me up. And I thank yourself as well." The traveler wiped his wet face with the back of his hand.

Jubal pumped the gear shift and turned the International back onto the highway. He glanced from the corners of his eyes at the hitchhiker. The man from the side of the road had a thick black beard that was tangled and beaded with water. His frame was long and skinny—his knees bumped the dash—and he had a powerful, athletic build. Like Jubal, he was dressed all in denim: Levis wet from the snow, a bluejean jacket that was worn and filthy, a blue work shirt.

Jubal offered his name and his right hand to shake. The traveler took Jubal's hand and held it, for a few moments wouldn't let go. His grip was intense and hurt some. He stared evenly at Jubal in the premature November twilight. "I was lost out there and I *prayed* for you, Jubal Scott. I prayed for you to come to me. I was in the snow and the blowin' wind and I prayed for someone to come and lift me out of it and here you are."

Only when he was done speaking did he let Jubal take his sore hand back.

"First time ever I been the answer to someone's prayers," Jubal said.

"You know not how you may be called to serve Him. You know not the way or the time."

"Yep. I expect you're right."

They went for a distance without speaking. It came to Jubal that the traveler had not mentioned his own name when they shook hands.

"How far am I taking you?" Jubal asked. "You headed some-wheres?"

"I couldn't tell you where it is I'm headed, because I don't know. I'm headed to where the Lord points me."

"Well. Good for you."

There was a rim of frost inside the glass of the windshield now, where the condensation had frozen, making pretty feathers of silver and chrome. Jubal reached out with one hand, scratched his fingertip at some of the frost.

"I can't believe this cold," Jubal said. "It was Indian Summer only two days ago. I hope you weren't out in it long."

"It was a terrible cold, but I didn't walk alone."

"Oh yeah? Was it Jesus walkin' with you?"

"He gave me His jacket," said the traveler. "I needed and He gave."

"I didn't know Jesus was such a fan of denims."

"You ought not to make fun of what you don't understand, Mr. Jubal Scott. He bled for you. He was bleedin' when I left Him. It's His blood on this jacket." He held up his left arm and Jubal saw the sleeve was covered in what seemed to be rusty dried blood, from cuff to elbow.

A few moments of silence passed between them. Jubal sat hunched at the wheel, the muscles in the back of his neck knotted and aching. A half-ton truck came over a rise and roared by them going the other way. For an instant its headlights filled the cab with white glare. Jubal glanced at his passenger, and saw what he hadn't when the man from the side of the road climbed into his truck in the dark. The front of his jacket was soaked in splashes of blood, dried and stiffened now. The traveler's right eye had an ugly purple-gray crescent around it and the eyelid was fatted. His lower lip gleamed with a shining slick of blood. What was most shocking was that his head was turned and he was staring openly at Jubal, allowing Jubal to see his bruised face. He was smiling—smugly. The truck blew past them, taking its light with it.

It was a bad thing to have seen. For a second Jubal was too rattled to speak, but the silences were threatening.

"It looks like He was really leakin'," Jubal said. "Did He give you that jacket, or did you take it off Him in a tussle?"

"They were the wounds of love."

"What about your face there?" Jubal asked, and swallowed. "Are them wounds of love too, or the old-fashioned hatin' kind?"

"I lost my way in the snow. I fell."

Get him out of the truck, Jubal thought, but he didn't slow down, and made no move to pull over. The traveler had his arms crossed over his chest, hands stuck under his armpits, and Jubal felt his gaze on him. In some way it felt important to his continued survival to keep driving. It likewise felt necessary to keep talking, not to show any alarm.

"Naw," Jubal said. "You were in a fight with someone. Probably over that jacket."

"If you don't believe what I'm saying to you, why don't you pull over and I'll get out."

Jubal was holding the wheel too tightly, but it was hard to loosen his hands. The countryside was black under the starless sky. He wished they would come on a town, or if not that, then he wished to see a single lit window in a farmhouse somewhere. But there was no town, and no farmhouse with lights in the windows. It was in his mind that the man from the side of the road had cut someone for the jacket.

The traveler might have a straight razor on him. Maybe if Jubal pulled over out here in the middle of the northern empty, the traveler would decide it was time for Jesus to supply him with a 1928 International in passing fair condition.

Jubal said, "I'll ride you a ways further. I wouldn't want to put any man out in this snow. Besides, if you had a fight with someone over that jacket or a bottle or something, I don't see how it's any of my business."

They passed two signs at the edge of the road. The first had the number 5 on it. The second said that the township of Bethel was only three miles away. There would be a place to let the traveler off in Bethel—there would have to be.

The man from the side of the road was turned in his seat and staring out the passenger window, and Jubal studied him for a moment, looking at him sideways. The thought would not stop going around and around in his head that the drifter had left some person, likely another derelict, in the falling snow and the freezing night with blood jugging out of him. There was a tightness in Jubal's chest that made it difficult to breathe. It was as if his shirt was a size or two too small and his chest couldn't expand the way it wanted to.

"If you were walkin' with Jesus, where'd He go when you got in with me?" Jubal asked, wondering if the traveler would say something that would reveal the condition of whoever he had slashed and left. The safest thing was to be maybe a little thick; to seem careless. Carelessness and courage were much the same thing in the winter dark. And it was only three miles more to Bethel. Jubal said, "I'm worried about Him is all. You said He was bleeding. This isn't any kind of weather to be staggering around in hurt. What was He doing the last time you saw Him?"

"The last I saw Him He was running beside the truck. Just a moment ago. Running at the side of the road," the traveler said. His head was leaned forward so his brow touched the passenger side window. Jubal saw steam from the traveler's breath spread over the glass. "He's gone now."

"Where'd He go, you figure?"

"To Heaven. For to take His rest." He did not turn or look at Jubal when he spoke now, but went on staring out the window. "When He sleeps parts of the world disappear. It's only because He wants it that it exists at all. Only because He is always thinkin' on it, because He wants it for us. It is a strain to Him to keep the world made. Only souls are permanent. All other substance is irresolute. It is in the nature of all other matter to weaken and lose shape, to forget what it was and what it was meant for. To spill and run. This has recently been proven by science. That all things are headed apart, everything running away from everything else, until there's nothing left of anything, just heat and a confusion of particles, and no difference at all between the particles that made men and the particles that made the things they fought over. Because it takes energy and spirit to hold things together, and it don't take nothing for things to come apart." The wind ran shrill through Jubal's cracked-open window. The traveler said, "Some of it out there goin' right this instant. Goin' and not comin' back."

The International reached the top of a hill, and Jubal saw on the bottom of the downslope a log tavern with trucks parked in the lot. The sight of the place filled him with such a strong sense of relief, he felt a little like laughing. He was not afraid of the traveler anymore, either, and also felt a little mean towards him for scaring him in the first place.

"There's somethin' hasn't gone away yet," Jubal said. "Hope it doesn't vanish before I get in there and get a drink."

He slowed and wheeled the truck into the lot, found a place to park the International that was close to the front door. Jubal looked across the seat at his passenger. "Well. I'm headed in. Buy you a cup of coffee if you want. I never met a man I thought could use it more."

Jubal wanted the man from the side of the road to come into the tavern with him. His courage was back now, and he wanted to know about the traveler's battered face and the blood on his jacket. Once he had him in the tavern, he thought he could see to it that the hitchhiker didn't leave until someone had put a call into the local sheriff. If the traveler had left someone slashed by the side of the highway, he might not be dead; he might yet be saved. For an instant Jubal had some cloudy ideas about himself as a hero, and cold oxygen swelled his lungs and his heart thudded a little faster.

"No, sir. I'll be on my way."

"Why don't you come on in?"

"I'll be going. I can see what you think of me. I can see how you want to laugh at me."

"Well come on in and ask around about a ride then."

"No thank you. I'll look for one by the road."

Jubal said, "Why won't you come in? On account of it's a barhouse? Why is it you big buddies with Jesus think the barhouses are full of sinners headed for Hell? Jesus never met a glass of wine he didn't like."

"Why do you want me to come in with you so badly?" Asked the traveler. His face was composed and thoughtful...but Jubal thought there was a clenchedness in his jaw, just the slightest suggestion of malice.

Jubal said, "How'd you get that blood on your jacket? Really. If you left someone bleedin' somewheres, you ought to know they could die out in this weather. Why don't you just tell me about who you left cut up and where. Then you can beat it and I can find out about gettin' them help."

"The only one dyin' nearby is you, Jubal Scott. Dyin' on the inside. Dyin' in the spirit. I'll pray for you, although you have shown me disrespect and mocked my faith. You want to know who is bleedin' and why? Jesus the Nazarene is bleedin' and you are one of the causes of it. You are the nails in his palms. His blood is on you Jubal Scott." He said these things in a tone of soft, commanding quiet.

"All right," Jubal said. "That's enough. You keep talkin' it won't be just Jesus's blood I got on me. I'm thinkin' about makin' both sides of your face match."

The traveler lifted two fingers as in a gesture of benediction, and opened his mouth to say more, but Jubal closed one hand into a fist and held the fist where the traveler could see it. He wanted now only to be rid of him. "No. Just get. Go on with yourself." If he saw a straight-razor, Jubal would jump out and run for the bar...but he wasn't sure the traveler had a razor, and if he did, Jubal thought probably he wouldn't use it here, with light streaming into the truck from the tavern windows. The two men could hear people talking inside, a woman's high-pitched and drunken laughter.

The traveler looked at the fist for a moment, then twisted in the seat, snapped open the door and dropped out.

Jubal watched him go from the front step of the tavern. The traveler ducked his head down and stuck his hands into his filthy jacket and crossed the road to the opposite side, through the big feathery flakes of snow. Jubal stood with his hands also in the pockets of his jacket, shivering, although whether from cold or relief he could not tell. He watched until he could no longer discern the traveler against the background of towering black firs, and then Jubal turned and entered the bar. It was dimly lit, crowded and noisy with happy conversation. Jubal couldn't imagine where all the people had come from. It seemed he had driven for an hour in the company of the lunatic, without coming across a single sign of life anywhere.

He got a Scotch and sank onto an empty stool, grateful not to have to stand. The Scotch opened a fan of heat in his chest, and between that and the warmth of the room, the cold soon began to drain out of him and left him feeling weak and boneless. He told some others at the bar about the hitchhiker—his audience two young men (one of them appeared barely fourteen), and a flushed and flabby woman who could have passed for William Taft's twin sister. She laughed at everything he said. Jubal was surprised, wouldn't have guessed his story was humorous; still, it was a pleasure to be listened to, and to be warm, and to have a Scotch. He told them about the hitchhiker's crazy talk and his blood-soaked jacket and battered face and waited for someone to say he should call the police. No one did.

"You think he killed someone?" Jubal asked.

"Probably," said one of the men, and the woman laughed so that her whole gelatinous body shuddered.

"He might've been workin' on a farm," said the fourteen-year-old. "He might've been cuttin' animals. My brother cut hogs for a week down in Fryeburg and come home every night lookin' like Jack the Ripper. He was savin' for things, but he quit. He said there isn't anything you need to have so bad you got to do all that."

"What about his bruised face?"

"Maybe he fell walkin' in the snow," said the boy.

Jubal said, "That's how he explained it."

"Well. There you go."

"So you comin' from Massachusetts?" asked the older man. "Where? Boston?"

"Worcester area actually."

"I ain't never been to Boston and don't never need to go," said the man. "They ain't got nothin' there I want."

Jubal nodded and wondered how late it was. Just the thought of standing up exhausted him. Surrounded by the friendly noise of the tavern, it was harder to believe the drifter had killed anyone. Jubal made eye contact with the bartender, who lifted his chin in acknowledgment and started his way. Jubal had it in mind to order a second Scotch, but before he could, someone walked past behind him, calling to a friend that the snow was really piling up outside. When the barkeep arrived in front of him, instead of ordering another, Jubal slid off the stool and asked him what was owed. He hoped for a benevolent reception at Linda's, and it wouldn't do to arrive too late in the night.

Jubal had thought he had got the last word in with the man-who-had-a-jacket-from-Jesus, but it turned out he had not. When he came outside, he found a bloody cross fingerpainted on the driver's side window. Another red cross was in the snow on the hood, and over it, in crooked, badly made letters was a single word: FORGIVE. Jubal wiped it all off with lumps of snow.

He drove on through the hilly town center of Bethel and into the lightless countryside again. The branches of trees, bony and bare of leaf, were tangled together in an archway over the road, and his headlights opened a tunnel beneath them. Streams of snow ran across the road in rivers of wedding-day silk.

Tess Hakeswell's farm was off Route 5 and along a narrow lane that wound up and down a series of low, stubby hills. Jubal had been there a couple of times before, once when he and Linda were still to-gether, once shortly after she moved there with Kelly. He sat in the truck and studied the farmhouse for a time. Two windows on the ground floor had lights in them. Through them Jubal could see into the front sitting room—although from the angle he had in his truck, all he could really make out of the sitting room was its upper half. He could see pale yellow wallpaper, and motionless sheets of cigarette smoke hanging in the air under the bare light bulbs. He knew from all the smoke that Tess at least was sitting in there with her knitting in her lap and a radio program on. Perhaps Linda was sitting and smoking with her.

He stared at the house, imagining the two of them sitting in that poison-colored fogbank of tobacco smoke...mostly imagining Tess. She was a small, wiry woman, with a purple birthmark shaped like an enormous arrowhead on her face. It started on her forehead, and fell across her right eye socket in a triangle, the tip of the arrow pointed at the ground. It was as if she had been born with a black eye that would never go away. Since her predominant mood was an attitude of sulking hostility, a permanent black eye seemed in some way just right. Jubal wanted to find a way to talk to Linda without Tess standing in the background. If he could get Linda outside, he thought he had a chance to start things off on the right foot. Inside, everything would be against him: Tess's knitting needles clicking together, the old stained wallpaper coming unpeeled from the walls, the harsh light of the naked lightbulbs.

Jubal was trying to settle on what he would say after Linda an-swered his knock, when a figure sat up from the snow in the front yard, only a few feet away. Jubal jumped a little behind the wheel. The person in the yard was a child, in burly jacket and mittens. The child had been lying in the snow sweeping her arms and legs back and forth to make a snow angel. Jubal also spied a nearby pyramid of snowballs, a snowman in a straw boater, and a small elm with the outer works of a snow fortress built around it; the work of many children. But the girl in the heavy jacket was alone.

He rolled the window down, his heart drumming in him with an uneasy force. He had not seen his daughter since she was three-going-on-four. She was backlit; he could see nothing of her face.

"Hey there, girl," he said. "Can you tell me is this the Hakeswell estate?"

The girl stood, dusted off her butt, and stepped carefully out of her angel. She picked up a snowball. Jubal wondered if he was about to be pelted, began imagining how Linda might have Kelly so turned against him that he was about to come under fire without so much as a word hello. But Kelly only stuck the snowball in her mouth and chewed on it while she came across the yard. She stopped five feet from the International.

"Who are you looking to talk to?" she asked.

"I was trying to hunt down my little girl. I heard she needed a sledding partner, and I was available for the weekend."

Her breath spilled white and cold from her lips. The hand with the snowball in it dropped to her side.

"You were only small the last time I got up this way. You haven't seen me in a while. Do you remember your old man at all? You forget my face?"

She didn't answer.

"Well. I got this truck now. I'm meaning to stop in more often. I feel bad it's been so long." He had not thought he would have to speak to Kelly first, and felt unprepared for the conversation—if this was a conversation. She had not spoke since he identified himself. He said, "You like this truck?"

She looked back at the house. "I should get Mom."

"I sent a letter saying I was going to come. Did your Mom tell you?"

She stared.

"She didn't?"

Kelly again looked over her shoulder at the house.

There would be time later to think about why Linda hadn't told Kelly he was coming. Jubal asked, "Are you unhappy to see me?" He smiled to take the edge off it, raised his hands, palms turned outward, as if in surrender. "You wanna bomb me with that snowball? That'd be all right. Wouldn't blame you."

She said, "I'm going to get my Mom."

"Kelly," he said. It startled him—he had never heard his own voice sound desperate before.

She turned and ran up the yard, but before she had even reached the front steps, Jubal saw the door open. In the yellow rectangle of the screen door stood two women silhouetted. Kelly clumped across the porch and stood on the other side of the screen. Jubal saw his daughter raise an arm and point a mitten at his truck. The screen door opened and one of the women put her hand on the back of Kelly's head, and nudged her inside. Then the woman came onto the porch and crossed her arms, hugging herself tightly, and started across the yard towards the truck.

Jubal sat with his hands in his lap, and watched her come quickly across the snow with her head down.

"What are you doing here, Jubal?" Linda asked. She wore just a thin dress.

The sharp tone of accusation in her voice made him suddenly timid and he forgot whatever it was he had planned to say. "Well, I come up to see Kelly like I said I was going—"

"Just leave," she said. "Just go away."

Linda was turned slightly, and he could see her face in the pale light from the house. It was a different face from the one he remembered. It was drawn, and there were thin lines at the corners of her eyes. The eyes themselves seemed a slightly different shade; not the deep blue he remembered, but faded, a color almost white.

"How's that fair?" he asked. "She's as much—"

"Fair? *Fair?*" she cried, her voice rising. "You don't want to talk to me about fair, Jubal Scott. I have put the clothes on her back, and the food on her table. When she had the German measles I was the one sat by her bed all night and prayed to God she wouldn't die—and you didn't even know she had 'em. What have you ever done for her? You think you can just come up like this, you haven't been to see her what in four years and—"

"You're up in the goddamn middle of nowhere goddamn it—which you did on purpose, just to get away from me. How was I supposed to come, with no ride, and no money?" Jubal heard the screen door slap, looked past Linda, and saw Tess with a coat thrown on over her nightgown, coming across the yard.

"You can't just appear out of nowhere for a couple of days, and then leave for another three years. I won't have you tease her with the idea she has a father," Linda said.

"I haven't come in the past because I couldn't. I didn't have any way. I got this truck now. I'm not here to tease her."

"What's he doing here?" Tess called out. She stopped ten feet from the truck. Her voice had the harsh, reedy sound of a crow cawing. "Send him away, Linda."

"I'm doing this, mother," Linda said. "Go in."

Tess Hakeswell didn't move. Backlit as she was, her face was dark; the violet birthmark around her right eye was even darker.

Jubal said, "Is that why you didn't tell her I was going to come up? Thought I was just going to tease her?"

"You've said you were going to visit a hundred times before, but you never once did."

"I never said I was visitin' before. I said I wished I could visit. There's a difference there, Linda. Just a little difference, but important."

"Don't smart-mouth off to me."

Tess cried out, in a shaking voice, "He's been drinkin', Linda. I can smell it from here. Send him away."

When Jubal looked past Tess and Linda, he could see Kelly standing inside the screen door. She was staring out at them, but with her mittens pressed over her ears.

"Go, Jubal. Go," Linda said. She turned away.

"And what do you mean, I never done anything for her? What about the money I sent? I always sent money whenever I—"

Linda wheeled back, and even in the poor light he could see the blood swell crimson into her face, and her voice shuddered. "*What? What money, Jubal? When?* Five dollars, last October, five stinking— what's that supposed to buy? Oh God, Jubal. Oh God. Drive away before I kill you. I mean it. I won't be able to stop myself. You don't know."

"I sent money more times than just that five dollars," he said, genuinely frightened now, leaning away from her.

"*When?*" she screamed. "Except for that five dollars you haven't sent nothin' since February."

"No," he said. "No, in the summer, in—"

"*February.* I remember because you put a feather in the letter, and it was February, and you haven't done a single thing for that little girl since then. You have to go, Jubal, I swear, you have to go right now—" and Linda spun away once more.

The truth of it—*February,* he thought, reeling inside—was almost more than he could stand. His temples pounded. He wanted more than anything to keep Linda from going. He reached through the window and caught her by the sleeve of her dress.

She turned back and hawked up a mouthful of spit and spat. It struck him above the left eye. He let go of her dress and jumped back, blinking, wiping his arm at his face. Linda staggered away from him, up the yard towards the porch, her breath coming in strangled sobs. He stared at her a moment, then looked over to Tess. The old woman was turned slightly so some light from the house fell on half her face, the half with the permanent black eye. The corner of her mouth was turned up in a thin-lipped smile.

"Are you happy with the work you done here tonight, Mr. Scott?" Tess asked.

"You want to take that grin off your face," he said to her, in a low and shaking voice. "Before I get out this truck and knock it off, you bony ol' cunt."

The color drained from her face, left her cheek waxy, and the arrowhead birthmark looking like a great splash of black ink. She turned and hurried after her daughter.

He drove back the way he had come without seeing. He was gripped now and then by a convulsion of anger; once he laughed unhappily, and touched his forehead where she had spat on him.

It was hard to string thoughts together. Just when he would start to try and sort his ideas out—to talk to himself about what had happened, or what he should have done—a fresh spasm of emotion would come over him, and he would be breathing hard, and swallowing thickly, and feeling that he might do something terrible to himself. Drive off the road into a tree, maybe. He didn't know where he was going. He had unclear ideas about what could remain of the life ahead.

It was at last snowing hard. The black boughs of the firs at the side of the highway were loaded down with heavy piles of snow. The road was white, the snow not even packed down, with tire-ruts dug in it where other vehicles had passed. After he had been driving for a time, there were not even other tire ruts ahead. Once, on a gradual turn, the back end of the truck slipped to one side and Jubal cried out in surprise.

He sat up, pulled himself close to the steering wheel. Jubal didn't notice the exact moment when he stopped thinking about Linda and Kelly and the ol' bitch. He didn't know precisely at what moment he started to listen to his pulse whamming in his ears. He didn't know when he became afraid of the road. He slowed down until he was doing barely twenty miles an hour, and still his worn tires skidded and slipped on the curves. Jubal couldn't see a yard past the front of the truck in all the snow and there were no streetlamps, nor were there houses or farms with comforting yellow lights behind frost-shellacked windows. Jubal decided he would pull over the first chance he saw... but no chance came. The toes of his left foot throbbed horribly from the cold. His right foot, still on the pedals, was the only part of him that remained warm, and that was uncomfortably warm, sore and hurting from the heat. He lifted his foot off the pedal now and then, to slow down on the curves, but also to give his foot a rest from the scorching iron; when he removed his boot from the pedal, it came up with a tacky ripping sound. The interior of the cab stank of boiled rubber—the sole of his boot starting to cook.

He passed a country church, saw just a glimpse of it through the flying snow, and he thought, good, I'm coming on a town. It was the last time he was sure he was still on the road. He had slowed to less than ten miles an hour. The headlights cast a wan, unhelpful light.

Jubal drove with his heart rapping high and fast in his chest until the moment he rolled past the low sapling of a fir tree on the left of the truck. He wouldn't even have noticed it, except that it was so close to the side of the truck he heard it slap the metal. He pressed his foot to the brake and stopped. Jubal rolled the window down and stuck his head out. He squinted into the snow, looked back. The sapling was pressed against the side of the International, close to the rear left hand wheel. He put the truck into neutral and climbed out. His boots sank into four inches of snow.

"Oh Christ," he said, and jerked off his watch cap and slapped it on his knee. He looked back the way he had come. The tires had left deep trenches in the unbroken snow. He looked the way the truck had been headed. Off to the right was the edge of the forest, the high black pines, the bare oaks. He had been following the forest line, assuming it followed the road, and had gone off into an unfenced field somewhere. He hadn't had any awareness of leaving the highway; no bump as the tires went over the embankment, no sensation of moving over uneven ground.

He put a foot on the running board and hauled himself back into the cab. He would have to run it in reverse, follow the tracks back until he found the roadbed again. He doubted he had wandered far from the highway.

Jubal sat with a hand on the wheel, twisted around at the waist to stare through the rear window. He backed for a time without coming across where he had left the road, and the further he went the more he began to speed up, in a hurry to be on the highway again. He was going almost twenty miles an hour in reverse, when the International slipped a little to one side, out of the tracks the tires had left in the snow, and hit a snow-buried boulder with a steely crunch. The impact threw Jubal forward, and the steering wheel punched into his chest, and drove all the air out of him in a barking cough.

He cursed and instantly threw it into first—no intention in him to even get out and see the damage—and stomped on the gas. The back tires whined. The front end of the truck slid about from side to side, without moving forward any distance. He threw open the door and climbed out again into the night.

The crash had knocked all the snow off the boulder, which was shaped not unlike an egg, half of it buried below ground. He had just clipped it with the right-hand side of the rear bumper; the corner of the bumper had been shredded to ribbons of silver confetti. The International had continued to travel backwards another foot, the rock grinding along the undercarriage, until at last the truck had stopped when the right rear tire thudded against it. The back end of the truck was sitting on the rock, hoisted a half foot into the air. The rear right tire was not actually on the ground.

Jubal put his shoulder into the rear of the truck and heaved, shutting his eyes with the strain, his boots sliding in the snow. The truck stayed perched on the rock. He stood up gasping, his face damp and cold. Blinked at icy sweat and flexed his hands. With some boards he could move it maybe. If he had two other men with him they could rock it loose.

He stood for a while at the rear end of the truck, shivering light-ly. He was going to have to leave it. Go back to the road, and catch a ride and come back for it in the morning. He took his cap off and whapped it on the smashed bumper. It stuck on a hook of torn steel, and when he yanked it loose, the hook ripped a long tear in the fabric.

He walked into the falling snow, placing his feet in the tracks left from his tires. Jubal walked for perhaps a full minute and then turned to look back, and behind him lay a whitish-blue rolling land-scape, and the falling snow that in the darkness could not be seen as white but instead seemed black and resembled flakes of ash, and the truck gone in it, and he had the bewildering idea that he would never see it again, and discarded the thought as absurd, only it turned out to be true.

Jubal walked along the tire tracks. Snow formed in his eyebrows. Flakes of snow sometimes flew in his eyes and stung. He crossed a long gradual slope of winter white, a blank, shapeless empty, and around him the snow fell, and the world of the real was erased as by the for-getfulness of God.

The road was out there—he knew that. If he kept walking, he would come across it soon enough. He did not look back again.

The trucker took him to North Conway, New Hampshire, and Jubal used what money as he had on a room at the White Mountain Motel. The next morning he paid a farmer with a Model T a fifty cent piece to drive him up and down the Roosevelt Trail, looking for the Interna-tional. They spent most of the afternoon traveling the white country. Jubal saw gentle, snow-smoothed hills, brilliant under the bitterly cold sky. He saw spruce trees buckling under the weight of the snowheaps laid on their branches. He did not see the truck.

"You sure you were on the Rosie?" the farmer asked. "I can think of lotser other ways into Conway than that road."

The farmer drove Jubal around until the twilight. Jubal left descriptions of the truck at country stores, and diners, and with the Oxford County Sheriff, let them know where he could be contacted in Massachusetts, and many among them reassured him it would turn up, someone would notice it in their field soon enough. Jubal never heard from any of them. Sunday it was snowing again, and he thought his chances of finding the truck in the bad weather poor, and worried if he stayed any longer he might return late and lose his job as well as his truck. That day he hitched a hundred and ten miles back home to Summerland.

John Tierney, the WPA foreman, invited him to share Thanksgiving at his house, with his wife and three little daughters. Perhaps Tierney felt sorry for him, his truck getting wrecked up in Maine and all, when Jubal had only had it for a few months. That was what Jubal said—that it had been wrecked. You could not very well tell people it had just disappeared; that the winter had laid claim to it.

After an evening of little girls shouting and cheering and singing at the dinner table, Jubal expected to see his daughter in his dreams, and was not disappointed. He was sitting in the truck again, and Kelly sat up out of an angel she had been making in the snow. He rolled down the window and called out to her, but she was frightened to see him, and said she had to get her mother. She got up and ran away from him again, except that this time there was no house to run to, nothing but the long white hills and the night. He turned the International around and rolled slowly after her, the truck floundering in the snow, casting sprays of white up before it to leap in the glare of the headlights like foam jumping from rough whitecaps before a boat. He drove following the boot holes she had left behind her in the snow, but was unable to catch sight of her again, as if she could travel through the drifts without any effort of any sort. Sometimes he passed little-girl angelshapes made in the snow. No tracks ever led to them. They appeared to have made themselves. The truck whined and labored in the deep powder. In time even Kelly's boot holes disappeared, and there was nothing but the white slopes, and the hiss of snow driven in glittering fans by the wind. He drove on without thought, or any emotion other than desperation, without any true hope of finding where she had gone, out in the snow and pines, alone but for the company of her cold and faceless angels.

The Hidden Honey

Sunni Brown Wilkinson

"African Tribesmen Can Talk Birds Into Helping Them Find Honey,"
    —The New York Times. July 22, 2016

In the woods of Mozambique, there is hidden honey
in the trees. Men below with their long, white

teeth and broad lips make a single sound and a little bird
goes hunting, racing to find bees' nests, to smell

again that sweetness. Meanwhile, at the end of my street
the Congolese refugees arrive. They ride their bikes past

rows of colorful houses, rainforest replaced by scrub oak
and suburbs, bonobos by common dogs. They yell *Welcome!*

when I arrive with old shoes and kitchen towels. Evening
at the water park, I hold the youngest in my lap

and slide, and each time he runs up again, shivering
in delight. His uncle says, *15 years in the camp, now here,*

his grandfather's red felt hat around town, that slow
artless pace of a man taking it in. It's not easy

for the birds—bee stings, the tangled, nearly
unreachable corners of the woods—but the hooked

beak is a weapon even the youngest can use.
The little one leaps from my lap, tries to slide down

alone, his tiny body churning in the water at the bottom
before someone dives in. He was born in a camp,

has traveled farther than any postage stamp
my sons have ever seen. After the men follow

the winged honeyguide and smoke out the trees
and take the honey, scientists say the birds

eat the wax. It's a pact between humans and birds
centuries in the making, each generation

teaching the next. I hear the news about shootings,
rafts tattered in the sea, the chaos that breaks

a hope we've dreamed of, delicate: a stirring inside
the trees, a sweetness so rich *it catches at the back of the throat.*

In Motion

first published in *Volume XVII*

Paulann Petersen

No. I don't know how a story works—
How tyrannies of time and space
reclaim the tailings, heap by heap,
of pretense and memory, how the narrative
seems to plead for a little violence,
a sharp edge swung against flesh,
and at the end, the story's bruise
rising to show its color.

To create character is, for me,
a process of complete mystery.
To make a *he* talk through lips of described
color and shape demands that a *she*
answer, commanding a plot
of alternate sympathies, a need
to tinker with verbs, to avoid
what simply *is*. A story's sentences
could then haggle for given proportion,
even set up housekeeping rules,
a strict division of labor.

I choose the alternative any day,
every day—a little aimless ramble
over fresh grass, my footprints
springing into disappearance behind me,
motion's sake making my way
into the poem's wild blank yonder.
Come what may.

Contributors

Darius Atefat-Peckham lives in Huntington, WV with his family. His work has appeared in venues such as *Brevity, Rattle, The Claremont Review,* and *Juxtaprose Magazine.*

Joe Ballard is a Marine Corps veteran who served two tours in Iraq. For his writing, Joe has been awarded the Binford Scholarship, honored as the Writer Laureate at Clackamas Community College, and has won creative writing contests up and down the Pacific Northwest. He is currently not sleeping while in pursuit of his undergraduate degree in Creative Writing at Marylhurst University. This is his first publication.

Bruce Barrow's stories have appeared in several print and online journals. He produces and edits television documentaries for Oregon Public Broadcasting and PBS.

Jude Brewer's work has appeared in *Scintilla, Cultured Vultures,* and now the *Clackamas Literary Review.* He hosts a film podcast, *John Plays the Piano,* and is currently finishing his anachronic dramedy memoir, *20 Bullshit Jobs I Needed.*

Charlene Logan Burnett earned an MFA in playwriting from UC Davis. Her work has appeared or is forthcoming in *Witness Magazine, Whiskey Island Magazine, Kestrel, WomensArts Quarterly,* and other magazines and journals. She was named a 2016 finalist in both The

Howard Frank Mosher Short Fiction Prize, sponsored by *Hunger Mountain*, and the Curt Johnson Prose Awards, sponsored by *December Magazine*. She is currently working on a novel and a collection of short stories.

Heather Anne Charton earned her MFA at Lesley University. She currently lives and writes in the backwoods of Northeast Ohio. Her work has also appeared in *Bird's Thumb* and *The Writer's Chronicle*.

Nick Conrad's poems continue to appear in national and international journals, most recently the Fall 2014 issues of *Orbis* (UK) and *Southern Poetry Review*, and the 2015 issues of *Badlands*, *Blast Furnace*, *Hawai'i Pacific Review*, and *Kentucky Review*. In 2016, his work appeared in *Stoneboat*, *The Cortland Review*, *Red Savina*, *Split Rock Review*, *Valparaiso Poetry Review* and *Coe Review*. Nick's work has been accepted for future issues of *Wilderness House Literary Review*, *Slipstream*, and *Mayday Magazine*. Other recent publications include issues of *Blueline*, *Borderlands*, *The Chariton Review*, *Colere*, *Dos Passos Review*, *Freshwater*, *Hawai'i Pacific Review*, *J Journal*, the *Kerf*, *South Carolina Review*, *Sow's Ear Poetry Review*, and *Stand* (UK). Recent anthology appearances include P & Q Press's *Bridging New York* and the Winterhawk Press Anthology, *Zeus Seduces*.

Fred Dale is a husband to his wife, Valerie, and a father to his occasional jerk of a dog, Earl. He is a Senior Instructor in the English Department at the University of North Florida, and is pursuing an MFA at the University of Tampa, but mostly he just grades papers. His poetry has appeared or is forthcoming in *Sugar House Review*, *Crack the Spine*, *Chiron Review*, *Dunes Review*, *Stirring*, and others. His audio chapbook, *The Sleep of Blue Moon Flowers*, was released through Eat in 2016.

Stephen Dobyns has published fourteen books of poems, twenty-three novels, a book of short stories, and two books of essays on poetry, the most recent, *Next Word, Better Word*, released by Palgrave in April, 2011. His most recent book of poems, *The Day's Last Light Reddens the Leaves of the Copper Beech*, was published by BOA Editions in 2016. His previous book of poems, *Winter's Journey*, was published by Copper Canyon in 2010. His most recent novel is *Saratoga Payback*, published in March 2017 by Blue Rider Press. It is the eleventh in a series of mysteries set in Saratoga Springs, NY. His new and selected poems, *Velocities*, was published by Penguin in 1994. Two of Dobyns' novels and two short stories have been made into films. His book of poems, *Black Dog, Red Dog*, was made into a feature length film in 2015 by James Franco. He has received a Guggenheim fellowship, three fellowships from the National Endowment of the Arts and numerous prizes for his poetry and fiction. His novel *The Church of Dead Girls* (Holt, 1997) was translated into twenty-three languages. Dobyns teaches in the MFA Program of Warren Wilson College; and in the past at Sarah Lawrence College; Emerson College; Syracuse University, where he designed and initiated the MFA program in creative writing; Boston University, University of Iowa and half a dozen other colleges and universities. He was born in Orange, NJ, in 1941. He lives in Westerly, RI.

Inspired by the colors, forms, and movement of her surroundings, **Alison Dougherty** channels her love of nature and curiosities for truth in order to evoke feelings of nostalgia and wonder. Her methods are both simple and technical. After a long, demanding career in commercial art and a shoulder injury from painting countless murals from the west coast all the way to Louisiana, life forced her to finally focus on her own art. She is the owner and artist of Outlier Gallery, a mobile art space she built inside a step van. You can follow her adventures on Instagram, Facebook, and twitter.

Okla Elliott is an assistant professor at Misericordia University. He holds a PhD in comparative literature from the University of Illinois, an MFA in creative writing from Ohio State University, and a certificate in legal studies from Purdue University. His work has appeared in *Cincinnati Review, Harvard Review, Indiana Review, The Literary Review, New Ohio Review, Prairie Schooner, A Public Space, Subtropics,* and elsewhere, as well as being included as a "notable essay" in *Best American Essays 2015.* His books include *From the Crooked Timber* (short fiction), *The Cartographer's Ink* (poetry), *The Doors You Mark Are Your Own* (a novel), *Blackbirds in September: Selected Shorter Poems of Jürgen Becker* (translation), and *Pope Francis: The Essential Guide* (nonfiction, forthcoming).

A writer and scholar, **Gustavo Pérez Firmat** is the author of several books of poetry, among them *Bilingual Blues, Scar Tissue,* and *The Last Exile.* He teaches at Columbia University, where he is the David Feinson Professor in the Humanities.

Kate Gray's passion is being a teacher, a writing coach, and a volunteer writing facilitator with women inmates and women veterans. She is the author of three poetry collections, and her first novel, *Carry the Sky,* stares at bullying without blinking.

Joe Hill is the #1 *New York Times* Bestselling Author of *The Fireman*, *NOS4A2*, *Heart-Shaped Box*, and *Horns* (which was made into a feature film starring Daniel Radcliffe). His book of short stories, *20th Century Ghosts*, won the Bram Stoker Award and British Fantasy Award for Best Collection. He earned the Eisner Award for Best Writer for his long-running comic book series, *Locke & Key*, featuring the eye-popping art of Gabriel Rodriguez.

Wynne Hungerford has published fiction in *Epoch*, *Talking River*, *The Whitefish Review*, *The South Carolina Review*, and *The Weekly Rumpus*, among other places. In 2013, she won The Meadowlark Award for her story "Ladies Chocolate Night." She is currently an MFA candidate at the University of Florida.

Stephen Graham Jones is the author of sixteen novels and six story collections. Most recent is the werewolf novel *Mongrels*, from William Morrow. Next are the comic books *My Hero*, from Hex Publishers, and *Mapping the Interior*, from Tor. Stephen lives and teaches in Boulder, Colorado.

Deborah Keenan is the author of nine collections of poetry; the three most recent are *Willow Room, Green Door: New and Selected Poems*, Milkweed Editions; a limited edition book from broadcraft press of writing ideas and options, *from tiger to prayer*; and, from Red Bird Chapbooks, a limited edition book, *so she had the world*, of 12 poems and 12 paintings by Susan Solomon. She is also the co-editor, with Roseann Lloyd, of *Looking for Home: Women Writing About Exile*, from Milkweed Editions.

Jeff Knorr was the Poet Laureate for the city and county of Sacramento from 2012–2016. Jeff is the author of four books of poetry, *The Color of a New Country* (forthcoming, Mammoth Books), *The Third Body* (Cherry Grove Collections), *Keeper* (Mammoth Books), and *Standing Up to the Day* (Pecan Grove Press). His other works include *Mooring Against the Tide: Writing Poetry and Fiction* (Prentice Hall); the anthology, *A Writer's Country* (Prentice Hall); and *The River Sings: An Introduction to Poetry* (Prentice Hall). His poetry and essays have appeared widely in literary journals and anthologies including *Chelsea, Connecticut Review, The Journal, North American Review, Red Rock Review, Barrow Street,* and *Like Thunder: Poets Respond to Violence in America.* Jeff Knorr lives in Sacramento, California, and is Professor of literature and creative writing at Sacramento City College.

Robert Kostuck is an M.Ed. graduate from Northern Arizona University. Recently published fiction, essays, and reviews appear in many American and Canadian print journals and anthologies. He is currently working on short stories, essays, and novels; his short story and essay collections seek a publisher.

Donald Levering's 7th full-length poetry book, *Coltrane's God,* was published in 2015 by Red Mountain Press. His previous book, *The Water Leveling with Us,* placed 2nd in the 2015 National Federation of Press Women Book Award. He is a past NEA Fellow in Poetry and winner of the 2014 Literal Latté Poetry Award, First Runner-Up for the 2015 Mark Fischer Prize, and finalist for the 2016 Ruth Stone and New Letters prizes. He has been a Duende Series Reader and was a Guest Poet in the Academy of American Poets online forum. More information is available at donaldlevering.com.

Margaret Malone is the author of the story collection *People Like You*, a Finalist for the 2016 PEN Hemingway Award, Winner of the 2016 Balcones Fiction Prize, and selected as a best of 2015 by Powell's Books, *The Oregonian*, *The Portland Mercury*, and elsewhere. A co-host of the artist and literary gathering SHARE, Margaret lives in Portland, Oregon, with her husband and two children.

Daniel Edward Moore's poems have been published in journals such as: *The Spoon River Poetry Review*, *Rattle*, *Assaracus Review*, *Columbia Journal Of Arts and Literature* and others. His work has also been nominated for a Pushcart Prize. His poems are currently at *Permafrost Magazine*, *Compose Literary Journal*, *Glint Literary Journal*, *Steel Toe Review*, *The American Journal Of Poetry*, *Coal Magazine*, *Gravel Magazine*, *Lullwater Review*, *Prairie Winds*, and *South Florida Poetry Journal*. He has poems forthcoming in *Common Ground Review*, *Tule Review*, *New South*, *Weber Review*, *Roanoke Review*, *Glass: A Journal Of Poetry*, and *December Magazine*. He lives in Washington on Whidbey Island. His book, *Confessions Of A Pentecostal Buddhist*, was just released on Amazon. Visit Daniel at Danieledwardmoore.com

Patricia Colleen Murphy founded *Superstition Review* at Arizona State University, where she teaches creative writing and magazine production. Her book *Hemming Flames* (Utah State University Press, 2016) won the May Swenson Poetry Award judged by Stephen Dunn. A chapter from her memoir in progress was published as a chapbook by *New Orleans Review*. Her writing has appeared in many literary journals, including *The Iowa Review*, *Quarterly West*, and *American Poetry Review*, and most recently in *Black Warrior Review*, *North*

American Review, Smartish Pace, Burnside Review, Poetry Northwest, Third Coast, Hobart, decomP, Midway Journal, Armchair/ Shotgun, and *Natural Bridge.* She lives in Phoenix, AZ.

Harry Newman's poetry has appeared in numerous literary journals over the last decade including *Rattle, Chautauqua, Ecotone, Asheville Poetry Review,* and *The New Guard,* among many others. His poems have been nominated for two Pushcart Prizes and shortlisted twice for the Bridport Prize in England. *Led from a Distance,* a collection of his political poetry, was published by Louisiana Literature Press in 2016. He can be contacted through his website www.harrynewman.com.

Naomi Shihab Nye's most recent books are *The Turtle of Oman* (a novel for elementary readers) and *Famous,* illustrated by Lisa Desimini. She has recently worked for the Sharjah International Book Festival in the United Arab Emirates and the Words Take Wing project through UC Davis.

Paulann Petersen, Oregon Poet Laureate Emerita, has six full-length books of poetry, most recently *Understory,* from Lost Horse Press. Her poems have appeared in many journals, including *Poetry, The New Republic, Prairie Schooner, Willow Springs, Calyx,* and the Internet's *Poetry Daily.* A Stegner Fellow at Stanford University, she received the 2006 Holbrook Award from Oregon Literary Arts. In 2013 she was Willamette Writers' Distinguished Northwest Writer. The Latvian composer Eriks Esenvalds chose a poem from her book *The Voluptuary* as the lyric for a new choral composition that's now part of the repertoire of the Choir at Trinity College Cambridge.

Born and raised in Nogales, Arizona, **Alberto Ríos** earned his BA and MFA in Creative Writing from the University of Arizona and holds the esteemed position of Regents' Professor at Arizona State University. His poetry, stories, and autobiographical work have been extensively published for nearly four decades. Among many other honors, Ríos has received the Walt Whitman Award in Poetry, the Western States Book Award for Fiction, and the Latino Literary Hall of Fame Award. In 2014, Ríos was elected to the prestigious position of Chancellor of the Academy of American Poets. During August of 2013, Rios was named Arizona's first state poet laureate, a position he held until 2015.

Matthew Roberson is the author of three novels, *1998.6, Impotent,* and *List.* He also edited the collection, *Musing the Mosaic: Approaches to Ronald Sukenick,* from SUNY Press. His short fiction has appeared in *Notre Dame Review, Fourteen Hills, Fiction International, Clackamas Literary Review, Western Humanities Review, McSweeney's Internet Tendency, Web Conjunctions,* and others. He has served on the FC2 Board of Directors since 2010.

Lee Rossi's latest book is *Wheelchair Samurai,* available from Plain View Press. Recent poems appear or are forthcoming in *Rattle, Spillway, Miramar, The Paterson Literary Review,* and *The Chariton Review.* He is a member of the Northern California Book Reviewers and a Contributing Editor to *Poetry Flash.*

Tim Schell's novel *Road to the Sea* was published in 2016, and he is the winner of the 2004 Mammoth Book Award for Prose for his novel *The Drums of Africa* which was published in the fall of 2007. In 2010, Tim's novel *The Memoir of Jake Weedsong* was The Finalist in the

AWP novel competition, and in 2011 it was published by Serving House Books. Tim's fiction has been nominated for a Pushcart Award and he was the winner of the Martindale Award for Long Fiction. Along with Jeff Knorr, Tim is the co-author of *Mooring Against the Tide: Writing Fiction and Poetry* (Prentice Hall, 2006) and the co-editor of the anthology *A Writer's Country* (Prentice Hall, 2001). Currently, he is the Chair of the Writing, Literature and Foreign Language Department at Columbia Gorge Community College in Hood River, Oregon.

Miranda Schmidt's work has appeared or is forthcoming in *The Collagist, Phoebe, Luna Station Quarterly, Driftwood Press*, and other journals. Miranda grew up in the Midwest and now lives with her partner and two cats in Portland, Oregon, where she edits the *Sun Star Review*, teaches at Portland Community College, and occasionally blogs about books at mirandaschmidt.com. A graduate of the University of Washington's MFA program, Miranda recently completed a novel about haunting and is currently at work on a project inspired by shapeshifting fairy tales.

Warren Slesinger is a former university press editor and publisher who lives in South Carolina where he explores its hills and marshes, and speaks to its people. With numerous publications of his poetry, he received a South Carolina Poetry Fellowship in 2002, and a collection of his poems and definitions, *The Evening Light*, appeared in 2011.

Lauren Smith teaches English at Delta College in central Michigan. Her work has appeared in *The Writer's Chronicle, Prick of the Spindle, New Madrid, Umbrella Factory, NewPages, Bookslut*, and *The Toledo City Paper*. In 2015, Cambridge Scholars Publishing included her essay, "When the Need Arises: Acting the Extrovert in Order to Teach," in the anthology *An Introvert in an Extrovert World: Essays on the Quiet Ones*. She recently contributed to *The Best Advice in Six Words*, a print collection from *SMITH* magazine's "Six-Word Memoir" series (her advice: "Don't poof your hair. Just don't."). She earned an MFA in nonfiction from Bennington College in 2010.

Don Thompson was born and raised in Bakersfield, California, and has lived in the southern San Joaquin Valley for most of his life. Currently the poet laureate of Kern County, he has been publishing poetry since the early sixties, including a dozen books and chapbooks. For more information and links to his publications, visit his website, San Joaquin Ink (don-e-thompson.com).

Zev Torres is a writer and spoken word performer whose work has appeared in numerous print and on-line publications including *Palabras Luminosas: Luminous Words*, *Literary Orphans*, Five2One's online publication *#thesideshow*, the *Suisun Valley Review*, and the Long Island Poetry Collective's *Xanadu*. His poetry was also included in the Spring, 2016 Poetry Leaves exhibition in Waterford, Michigan. Since 2008, Zev has hosted Make Music New York's annual Spoken Word Extravaganza, and in 2010 he founded the Skewered Syntax Poetry Crawls.

Julie Weston continues to write Idaho stories and has three published books: *The Good Times Are all Gone Now: Life, Death and Rebirth in an Idaho Mining Town* (University of Oklahoma Press, 2009) and two mysteries set in 1920s central Idaho, *Moonshadows* and *Basque Moon* (Five Star Publishing, 2015 and 2016). She lives in Hailey, Idaho, with her photographer husband, where they ski, write, photograph, and enjoy the outdoors.

Tyler Wilborn is a writer originally from Colorado Springs, Colorado. His work has appeared in the *The West Wind*, Azusa Pacific University's student-run publication, and *Kaaterskill Basin Literary Journal*. For more information on Tyler, please visit tylerwilborn.com.

Sunni Brown Wilkinson's poetry has been published or is forthcoming in *Sugar House Review, Rock & Sling, Tar River Poetry, Southern Indiana Review*, and other journals and anthologies and has been nominated for two Pushcarts. She is also the recipient of the Sherwin W. Howard Poetry Award from *Weber: the Contemporary West*. She holds an MFA from Eastern Washington University, teaches at Weber State University, and lives in Ogden, Utah, with her husband and three young sons.

John Sibley Williams is the editor of two Northwest poetry anthologies and the author of nine collections, including *Disinheritance* and *Controlled Hallucinations*. A seven-time Pushcart nominee, John is the winner of numerous awards, including the Philip Booth Award, American Literary Review Poetry Contest, Nancy D. Hargrove Editors' Prize, Confrontation Poetry Prize, and Vallum Award for Poetry. He serves as editor of *The Inflectionist Review* and works as a literary agent. Previous publishing credits include: *The Yale Review, Midwest Quarterly, Sycamore Review, The Massachusetts Review, Poet Lore, Saranac Review, Arts & Letters, Columbia Poetry Review, Mid-American Review, Poetry Northwest, Third Coast, Baltimore Review, RHINO*, and various anthologies. He lives in Portland, Oregon.

The *Clackamas Literary Review* is typeset in Sabon LT Std, an old-style serif designed by Jan Tschichold, and in Optima, a humanistic sans-serif designed by Hermann Zapf, and printed on 50 lb. white paper. Editing and design done by English Department students and faculty at Clackamas Community College, in Oregon City, Oregon.

Visit

CLR
CLACKAMAS LITERARY REVIEW

clackamasliteraryreview.org
clackamasliteraryreview.submittable.com
facebook.com/clackamasliteraryreview
@clackamaslitrev

Contact
clr@clackamas.edu

CLACKAMAS LITERARY REVIEW

the finest writing for the best readers

Clackamas Literary Review has been committed to publishing quality writing from around the world since 1997. Use the form below or visit us on Submittable to receive the latest and forthcoming issues.

Clackamas Literary Review

_____	1 year	$12
_____	2 years	$22
_____	3 years	$32

Name _____

Address _____

City / State / Zip _____

Email _____

Send this form and check or money order to:

Clackamas Literary Review
English Department
Clackamas Community College
19600 Molalla Avenue
Oregon City, Oregon 97045

www.ingramcontent.com/pod-product-compliance
Lightning Source LLC
Chambersburg PA
CBHW061954170626
46813CB00006B/2637